"You ever see the movie Crocodile Dundee?"

"You mean the one where Dundee whips out a knife the size of a machete?" Nathan imitated pulling the weapon out of a sheath.

"Exactly!" She trudged forward. "I'm wishing for that monster knife right about now."

"I'm thankful you don't have it," Nathan responded, staying a step behind her. "You'd end up using it on me in some misguided idea that I've wronged you."

Who knew Nathan Porter had a sense of humor? "Nothing misguided about my judgment, mister."

"Riiiiiight," he drawled. "Isn't using a machete a little bloodthirsty for Ms. Sunshine?"

"Depends," she puffed, wiggling between two tree trunks, scraping her calves on the bark. "We talking about using it to clear the vegetation or—"

Thunder reverberated, slicing through her eardrums and convulsing the ground. She threw her arms out to keep from falling just as lightning cracked, exploding in a deafening pitch. Light hurtled toward the earth, sparks flaring across her vision. Pressure hit her as a massive clap filled the thick air.

"Reena!"

P.A. DePaul resides outside Philadelphia in the US. In her free time you can find her reading, working on a puzzle, playing with her dog, winning game nights against her husband (sometimes) or whipping up something in the kitchen. You can learn more about her at padepaul.com, Facebook.com/padepaul and Instagram.com/padepaul.

Surviving the Storm

P.A. DePaul

LOVE INSPIRED
INSPIRATIONAL ROMANCE

LOVE INSPIRED®
INSPIRATIONAL ROMANCE

Recycling programs for this product may not exist in your area.

ISBN-13: 978-1-335-42703-8

Surviving the Storm

Copyright © 2022 by Penni DePaul

This edition published by arrangement with Harlequin Books S.A.

For questions and comments about the quality of this book, please contact us at CustomerService@Harlequin.com.

Love Inspired
22 Adelaide St. West, 41st Floor
Toronto, Ontario M5H 4E3, Canada
www.LoveInspired.com

Printed in U.S.A.

Be strong and of a good courage, fear not, nor be afraid of them: for the Lord thy God, he it is that doth go with thee; he will not fail thee, nor forsake thee.
—*Deuteronomy* 31:6

I dedicate this book to my husband.
You are my partner and best friend.
My rock and shelter in a storm. And a man
who makes this journey called life so much fun.

Acknowledgments

A huge thank-you goes to my husband, who took
multiple research hikes with me in the Poconos
and listened to (endless) hours of story ideas and
constant questioning of "What if..."

A massive hug and thank-you to the bestest agent
in the universe, Michelle Grajkowski.
Your warm heart and tireless cheerleading
keep this writer on the sane side of life.

A colossal thank-you to my editor,
Johanna Raisanen. Your guidance and feedback
have lifted this story way beyond where it started.
THANK YOU!

And last, but NEVER least, thank you to *you*,
the reader. You cradling this book in your hands
means the world to me.

Chapter One

"Listen up, everyone." Reena Wells raised her voice to compete with the group of teens and chaperones forming a loose circle in the dirt clearing. She couldn't stop the broad smile splitting her lips or keep her heels from bouncing. "We've made it to the second stop on our hike for the day, so that means—"

"Scavenger hunt!"

Squawk! Squawk! Squawk! The blast of twelve teenage voices startled the birds in the surrounding trees. Their cawing and flapping wings let everyone know how much they did *not* appreciate the disturbance.

Reena laughed. "And here I thought you'd be groaning to nap after this last stretch of uphill climb or complaining about the lack of cell phone signal."

"You haven't been listening to my uncle, then," Ashleigh Porter joked dryly, thumbing toward the good-looking man beside her, towering over her by a foot.

Said uncle snapped his spine straight; his cheeks, already red from exertion, deepened in color as he mock scowled at his niece. "Et tu, Brute?"

Ashleigh rolled her eyes and knocked her shoulder

into her uncle's bare biceps playfully. "No Shakespeare during summer break. It's a rule."

"Definitely," sixteen-year-old Rachel groused dramatically. "If I have to read another book filled with thees and thous, I'll—"

"Enjoy every minute of it," Sandy cut in sternly, shooting her daughter a look. Not surprising, given the mother was the high school English teacher.

Nathan Porter dropped a tanned arm over Ashleigh's shoulders and pulled his niece in for a side hug. Her gaze flicked to the ground, but Reena caught the slice of pain mixed with relief. A small pang twisted Reena's heart at the tragedy the fifteen-year-old had suffered six months ago. Having never known her mother, who died during childbirth, was already tough, but losing her father in a freak construction accident was horrible. Luckily, Nathan had uprooted his life from Virginia to their small town of Bell Edge, Pennsylvania, nestled in the Pocono Mountains, to raise Ashleigh on his own. To see them freely affectionate hit a soft spot inside.

"All righty." Reena clapped to halt her constant curiosity about the rugged man. Proffering a sheaf of green-colored papers, she continued, "Here's the items to find." Greedy hands snatched the pages and the mix of girls and boys, ranging from fourteen to seventeen, huddled into groups to study the list and the map showing the search area.

Stuffing the extra copies into the front pocket of the backpack resting at her feet, Reena soldiered on. "Remember, only pictures on your cell phones are needed as proof. We're not out to damage the environment."

By this point, she had only a few of the adults' attention. The kids were already trash-talking and making bets on who would complete the hunt first.

"What's the prize?" Vincent Clark, sixteen-going-on-sixty, asked, spearing Reena with serious eyes. A look that rarely left the boy's face.

All the chatter stopped and every gaze snapped to Reena. "Prize?" She screwed up her face in confusion. "I'm supposed to give out prizes?"

A few teens groaned and most of the chaperones snickered.

Rocking from toes to heels, she placed her hands over her heart. "How about my praise of a job well done?"

The boos that assaulted her made her laugh. "Wow, tell me how you really feel." She waited a few beats, then lifted her chin. "Fine, you bunch of ingrates," she mock insulted. "The first team back with the complete and correct list will not have to set up their own tents tonight."

Whoops and fists filled the air.

"The second-place team," Reena shouted, then lowered her voice as everyone quieted, "will not have to gather wood for the cooking fire. And the third-place team will not have to wake up early to cook breakfast." As director of the church's teen youth group, she avidly watched every penny and tried to find ways to save money so she could take the kids on more outings. Not handing out physical prizes cut costs and preserved her spine from schlepping them up the side of a mountain.

The level of noise rose to eye-popping as the kids chose teammates and continued egging each other on or predicting who'd win which prize.

"Everyone has chosen their team of four?" Reena asked, inspecting the newly formed groups.

"How much interaction are chaperones allowed to have

in the search?" Nathan asked, peering between Reena, his niece, and Vincent, who was now standing beside Ashleigh along with two other teens, Rachel and Andy.

"None," Reena answered.

Nathan's dark brown eyes narrowed. "None as in no pointing out items or—"

"None as in chaperones aren't going out with the teams." At Nathan's darkening expression, Reena hurried to explain. "This is about team building and fellowship with nature. Learning by experience is the best way to teach instead of adults hovering—"

"But it's dangerous in the forest," Nathan cut in, straightening to his full six-foot-two height. Ashleigh cringed and shot a look to her friends. "Someone could get lost or hurt."

"True," Reena agreed, doing her best to maintain an air of calm and authority. "But that's kind of the point. Kids need to learn how to handle those situations for themselves without an adult swooping in and doing everything for them. Besides—" she rushed to head off Nathan's next protest "—it's a small search area and I've included a map. Everyone will be fine. We have to trust the teens are old enough and intelligent enough to handle a simple scavenger hunt."

"Uncle Nathan," Ashleigh hissed. "I'll be *fine*. Since you obviously don't trust *me*. I'll be with the others. Promise." Her hand swished to indicate the other three in the team.

Nathan winced and scratched the brown scruff adorning his jawline. After swiping the same large hand through his multi-hued brown hair, leaving path marks in the waves, he dipped his chin once.

Ashleigh blew out an audible breath while Reena exhaled as silently as she could. She understood Nathan's hesitancy. Having lost his only brother and suddenly becoming responsible for a teenager could not be easy, but he couldn't keep a stranglehold on the girl if he didn't want to lose Ashleigh in the long run.

Scanning the rest of the group, she allowed the beauty of the lush scenery and the thrill of the fun challenge to flush out the tension tightening her muscles. "You've got forty-five minutes to return back here, whether you found everything or not."

Flushed faces beamed at her as some lowered into stances set for maximum takeoff.

Raising her arm, Reena shouted, "Happy hunting!" Dropping her fist, she pulled in her extremities as the teens raced past.

The presence of a dark cloud slowly blotting out the sun couldn't be ominous or a harbinger in any way, right?

Chapter Two

❧

Nathan Porter scrubbed his scruffy face with both hands, then grimaced at the dirt he'd just ground in. He sighed and dropped his arms. Not like he wasn't used to being grimy. Running electricity on construction sites and renovations as an electrical engineer had him anxious for a shower at the end of every shift.

A bird warbled and another answered somewhere overhead. Off in a distant clearing, the other adults rested, but he had wandered away shortly after the teens cleared out.

Stopping his meandering along a narrow trail, he stared at the jagged bark on a wide tree trunk until it blurred. What was he doing here?

He couldn't swallow past the sudden lump in his throat, and his lungs refused to fill. Grief slammed into him so hard, he bent at the waist with his hands on his thighs.

"Why?" he wheezed.

Why did his only brother, Scott, have to die? Dropping his head, he surrendered to the anguish sweeping through his body like a hurricane.

Losing the fight to remain upright, he crouched and

cradled his face. The others talked so freely about God and His benevolence, but Nathan couldn't understand how a *benevolent* God could take his brother away from Ashleigh. From him. From their parents. How depriving a fifteen-year-old girl of her father after already losing her mother was part of some overall plan. How Nathan was supposed to be okay with accepting that pithy excuse and move on. None of this was okay. Ashleigh needed Scott—

The terrifying and crushing weight of responsibility toppled Nathan forward. He caught himself with his hands and the forest debris dug into his exposed knees.

A guardian. Him. He knew *nothing* about raising kids, let alone being accountable for a hormonal, grieving girl. Ashleigh needed a woman to guide her, not a thirty-two-year-old bachelor whose longest relationship had lasted a year. And even that one had been on and off throughout the twelve months.

"God…" he choked. He couldn't decide if it was a plea, an outlet for the anger swirling among the pain, or a waste of breath. Maybe all three. He'd never had a strong foundation of faith, and losing Scott had him questioning the small piece that remained. The only reason he'd attended church every Sunday the past six months was for Ashleigh. She loved it and he'd do anything to keep her happy and healthy. Too many times he wondered if she was processing her father's death, and Lord knew Nathan had no clue what to do if she wasn't. Keeping her surrounded by her supportive friends felt right, so he kept going despite how much he wanted to stay home.

This weekend was just another example of his bumbling to do the right thing. A large part of him signed up as a chaperone to ensure nothing happened to her, but another part wanted to share an adventure that went beyond their burgeoning daily routine. Camping sounded good, but he couldn't see past the danger. He kept noticing all the ways his niece could end up in the hospital, or worse, lying in a grave beside Scott. And it'd be his fault for not protecting her.

"Dear God…" Squeezing his eyes shut against the horrific image, he inhaled the varied scents of the forest. No. He refused to lose Ashleigh, too. With that declaration, the outside world invaded his senses. Birds chirped and wings flapped, and small animals foraged to find food or items for their nests. If he didn't head back soon, someone was going to come looking. And now was not the time to lose it. He had to remain strong for his niece.

Slowly rising, he brushed the dirt and small twigs from his skin. He had a plan. Well, it wasn't really a plan. More a renewed determination to ensure nothing happened to Ashleigh. A vow to his brother that Scott's trust in naming Nathan as Ashleigh's guardian hadn't been misplaced.

Trudging back toward the clearing, he rubbed his bruised heart and hoped the others would keep their intrusive questions at bay. As the new—albeit reluctant—parishioner of the church, it didn't take a rocket scientist to guess they'd want to know everything about him. That wouldn't bother a typical person, but Nathan didn't have the capacity right now to let anyone else close. He was just barely handling this new direction in his life, and Ashleigh had his full focus. So far, during services, he'd managed to deflect and dodge, but in this setting he wouldn't get away with that for long.

His thoughts narrowed to the worship weekend's teen leader, Reena Wells. She captivated him as much as she frustrated him. She couldn't be much younger than his thirty-two years in age but, in spirit, he felt fifty years older. Kids and adults gravitated toward her whenever she walked into a room and she was always smiling as if life was one big joyride instead of hardships and trials. Even he found himself wanting to move closer, but managed to quell the urge. With dark auburn hair and big hazel eyes that twinkled, he always felt compelled to ask for the reason they sparkled. And don't remind him of her animated laugh that tickled his eardrums. He knew it was only a matter of time before he lost the battle against her gravity. He just needed it to be months and months from now.

Tiny claws scrabbling up a tree thankfully ended his musings about a complication he didn't want to invite into his life. Squirrels chased each other and chittered as they dashed around and up the trunk. Peering at the leafy canopy, he gawked. Whoa. Thick, dark clouds quickly covered the once blue sky, making the forest feel like the setting of a horror story. The dirt path, strewn with twigs and pieces of dead branches, snapped beneath his worn work boots while dried leaves skittered and swirled in the increasing wind.

The moving air swiftly compressed the sweat beading his neck and he shivered. He should have worn jeans instead of cargo shorts. His gut had warned him to cover his skin against nature but the muggy July heat had overridden his common sense.

"Nathan."

He snapped his eyes off the ground and settled on the man who coached soccer for the intramural league in his spare time. Tom had one of the coolest jobs in town. He was a conductor on the old-time railroad train that carried tourists through a scenic section of the mountain.

"I wondered if we were going to have to search for you." Tom clapped Nathan on the back, almost sending him to the ground.

"Nah." Nathan subtly moved out of range and stopped at the edge of the group. "I didn't go that far—"

"Well, it's official." Reena grimaced at the outdated weather band radio blasting a message among the static. She toggled a switch to silence the tinny voice droning through the single plastic speaker. "The storm's closing in on us instead of tracking south like forecasted."

Mouths tightened and worried gazes flittered to each other.

"We continuing on?" Sandy, the English teacher mom, asked, shifting toward the sound of thumping footsteps hurtling their way.

"Give it up, Patrick!"

"No way, Mitch," Patrick shot back, spurting forward into a flat-out run toward the adults. "I'm winning this hunt."

Mitch, followed closely behind by a herd of teens, increased his speed, coming within touching distance of Patrick, but not fast enough. Reena jumped to the side as Patrick slammed to a halt right where she had stood. Shoving his phone at her, Patrick crowed and hopped, performing some kind of victory dance that had zero coordination but a lot of enthusiasm.

Chaos reigned as teens jostled to have their lists checked and ensured they were ranked first through third place correctly. Others dashed to backpacks for water bottles and rags as they gulped water and wiped off dripping sweat coating their faces.

Nathan couldn't help but chuckle at their antics. These kids knew how to have a good time without the internet.

He'd give them that. It helped smother the anguish still clinging to his soul. Shuffling to the left, he craned his neck, looking for signs of Ashleigh among the herd, but didn't spot her chestnut hair swinging in a ponytail or her blue-based cross-trainers.

Six, seven, eight. He counted heads but came up short. "Anyone seen Ashleigh or the rest of her team?" he called over the voices, hoping someone would hear him.

Blank looks and shaking heads answered him.

His stomach tightened and he strode toward the path the kids had come from.

"Nathan, wait." A soft hand clasped his forearm, halting his progress. Reena.

"She could be hurt." The thought closed his throat and he struggled to swallow.

Reena moved in front of him, the top of her head just reaching his chin. "They're only a minute late. That's not really surprising when trekking through the woods."

Images of Ashleigh holding a broken foot or trapped between rocks assaulted his mind, ramping up his blood pressure.

Stepping into his space, a subtle scent of strawberries competed with his raging imagination of Ashleigh's potential injuries. "Give them at least ten minutes," Reena appealed, her large hazel eyes imploring him to listen. "Please."

Everything in him wanted to charge forward, but a small voice inside kept saying that Reena was right. Teens weren't known for punctuality. And being off in the forest with no chaperones was a perfect chance for them to lose track of time.

A roll of thunder echoed overhead, silencing the animals and insects.

"Reena?" the English teacher mom called, anxiety clear in the tone.

An up-swelling of ozone choked the air, warning of an impending downpour—

Right now. What little light the dark clouds allowed was impeded by rain assailing everyone and everything.

Shrieks and cackles became the new chorus as teens and adults scrabbled to dig out raincoats and shelter beneath their backpacks.

The warmth of Reena's hand encircling his forearm again clashed with the cool rain soaking his clothes, holding him from moving forward.

"We're going to have to postpone the rest of the trip," Reena shouted, the cacophony of nature almost drowning her out. "It's too dangerous to camp in the storm."

As if to punctuate her point, sticks of lightning tore across the sky.

Ashleigh. He had to find her.

"Sandy and Tom, can you lead everyone down to the parking lot?" Reena continued, obviously not keyed in to Nathan's mounting need to flee into the forest. "Shelter in the van. The keys are in the front pocket of my backpack."

Tom fished out a set of keys with an imperfect wooden cross, as if made by a youth in wood shop.

"What about you?" Sandy asked.

"And Andy, Ashleigh, Vincent, and Rachel?" a seventeen-year-old boy bundled in a red raincoat with the high school logo embossed on it asked, crowding closer.

"Reena!"

The high-pitched shout cut through the discussion, followed by another crack of thunder.

Whirling, Nathan spied Rachel running toward them

with Andy right behind her. The kids were soaking wet, spattered with mud, and terrified, if the looks on their faces were any indication.

"Ashleigh," Nathan barked, intercepting the kids. Blood roared in his veins and he had to hold himself back from grabbing them. "Where's Ashleigh?"

Tears poured down Rachel's cheeks and Nathan's lungs froze. No. No. No. Dear God. *No.*

"I don't know," Rachel croaked.

"We got separated." Andy clutched his left arm at the elbow as if attempting to hold back his trembling.

Lightning flared across the sky.

Rachel began babbling about splitting up to find the items faster, how it was so hot, she and Andy took a dip in the river, how Ashleigh and Vincent never met them at some pile of rocks, how they looked but couldn't find them... Nathan could barely follow the stream of words gushing forth.

"Rachel, breathe, honey." Sandy hugged the distraught teen.

Reena marched to her backpack, shoved the radio inside, then hoisted it onto her back. "Everyone, head back to the van as quickly and safely as you can."

"No way—"

"Nathan and I—" Reena cut his protest off "—are going after Ashleigh and Vincent."

Chapter Three

The rain fell so hard, Reena could barely see two feet in front of her. She wished she had taken a moment to put on her raincoat before she'd left the clearing, but she couldn't stop now. Her navy blue T-shirt with the youth group logo hung heavy and her athletic bicycle shorts that were supposed to wick away moisture lost the battle.

Mud caked her calves and coated her hiking boots. The once pleasant dirt path had turned into puddle palooza with detritus in all shapes and sizes waiting to trip her.

Nathan clomped beside her, tension radiating from his pores. From the set of his jaw, she figured he wanted to break into a run, but held back to maintain pace with her. A good thing. Her short legs would never keep up with his and the deep rivulets cutting into the mud made walking treacherous. The last thing they needed was a twisted ankle or broken leg. With spotty-to-no cell phone service, it'd be almost impossible to call for help.

"Tell me you have an idea where they are," Nathan's deep voice rumbled. The drenching rain plastered his hair to his head and his clothes to his physically fit body.

Thunder cracked and rolled, followed by streaks of lightning.

"I'm headed to the search area," she responded, hopping over a dead branch perpendicular to the path, "where most of the items on the list are located."

The corners of Nathan's mouth tightened and he studied her face a moment before turning away.

Wait a minute. Did he blame her for his missing niece? A shiver rippled through her gut. Was it her fault? Nathan hadn't wanted to let his niece go alone but Reena had thought him overprotective—

Nope. No way. "You can't seriously be blaming me."

"I can't?" His boot slammed into a puddle, spraying them both.

"No." Reena childishly stomped into a deeper puddle, sending up plops of mud to add to their misery.

"I told you it was dangerous."

"You have no idea what happened." Reena's breath came in pants, practically jogging to keep up with his increased speed. "For all we know, they went swimming, too, and are waiting out the storm like sane people."

He grunted. "Or they could be hurt and unable to get back to the clearing."

She couldn't really argue that point. It had been rolling through her mind from the start. She had just been resolutely pushing it aside in favor of concentrating on the positives. "You're overreacting—"

"I'm responsible for that girl's safety," he shot back. "Me. Not you."

"You're going to suffocate her if you don't loosen your grip."

He halted in the center of a crossroads. "Do you have kids of your own I haven't heard about?"

Ouch. Direct shot. Lifting her chin to bluff out the hit, she met his gaze. "No, but that doesn't mean I don't know what I'm talking about."

"It's way different when all the responsibility rests on your shoulders." He slapped his hands on his hips. "Where every decision you make has consequences, good or bad." A flash of pain overtook his brown eyes. "My brother..." He cleared his throat and swallowed hard. "Scott entrusted me..."

Pangs thumped through Reena's heart, responding to the grief surrounding him.

He lifted his sight to the treetops, then inhaled, visibly closing off his emotions behind a veil. "Ashleigh is all I have left of Scott and I mean to live up to his trust in raising her."

Reena's heart bled at the sorrow he locked behind a palpable imposing wall.

His gaze flitted over her face. "You live in a world full of sunshine and rainbows. Everyone is happy and optimism reigns, but I live in a far different space."

Why did he make it sound like her favorite traits were bad things? "Just because I refuse to obsess about every negative thing and worry about what *might* happen doesn't mean I don't live in reality."

He shook his head. "We don't have time for this argument. Which way?" He motioned to the two paths in front of them.

Marching onto the left fork, she muttered, "We wouldn't have to argue if you weren't so insistent that only you know what's best."

"I only insist—" he tossed the words to the back of her head "—because I *am* right."

Figured he'd heard that. A faint headache pulsed from the rain constantly pounding against her skull.

Trees swayed in the cold wind from the sudden temperature drop, ripping leaves off the branches and wheezing eerily. Foreboding crept down her spine; the storm seemed to be getting stronger.

Now was not the time to lash out because she was uneasy and riddled with apprehension. Allowing him to catch up to her, she shot him an overly sweet smile. "Since one of us needs to be the adult, I'll refrain from pointing out that not everyone has your control issues."

"You refrained from pointing that out, huh?"

"Yep." She widened her innocent smile. "Wasn't that—"

She cut herself off and Nathan stepped closer.

"What?" he asked, searching the area, then stiffening.

Trapped against the trunk of the tree was a soggy green-colored piece of paper with black ink running down the surface. Another blast of wind tore it off the tree and flipped it into the air. It soared, dipping and flipping as it sailed, to disappear out of sight.

"What is that sound?"

Reena cocked her head, then dread welled from deep within. Scrutinizing the area, she only now realized how far they had marched. Arguing with him had left her unaware of her surroundings. *Stupid, Reena.*

"It's the rapids," she answered hoarsely, the foreboding growing stronger.

The little bit of color Nathan had left drained from his face. "This river has rapids?"

In lieu of answering, she crashed through the forest. Unheeding every rule she'd ever learned about trekking safely across the uneven terrain, she plowed forward.

"Umph." Footsteps thumped behind her as well as the audible struggle against the dense vegetation. "Ow." Nathan kept right on her heels.

The tree trunks eventually thinned to only inches wide, while the varied vegetation grew thicker. More light chased away the oppressiveness as the thunder overhead competed with the roar of the river directly in front of them.

"Stop!" Reena threw her arm out like a soccer mom, but it was too late.

Nathan slammed into her, wrapping his arms around her backpack and chest, lifting her up. Pivoting on a dime, her feet flew up as he swung right to take a few steps along the side of the water.

The thrill that shot through her stomach at the sudden turn made her want to giggle while the angry rapids swelling the banks made her cringe.

"Sorry about that," Nathan panted, setting her down.

"No problem," she replied a little bit more huskily than she intended. Something red across the water caught her attention. "There. See that?"

Nathan followed her pointing finger and nodded. "Could be Vincent's high school jacket." He inhaled audibly. *"Ashleigh!"*

Reena's eardrum rang with the bellow. "The bridge's this way."

Nathan didn't wait. He took the lead, running and jumping over rocks and debris, and dodging the water swelling higher up the banks. *"Ashleigh!"*

Lightning forked across the sky and Reena trembled, praying it didn't decide to strike the water that kept lapping over her boots. A crack of thunder boomed, shaking the trees. The river raced past them, slamming against jutting stones and gobbling anything in its way.

"Is this thing safe?" Nathan shouted, but didn't slow. He pounded across the sopping wooden bridge that had been there longer than Reena had been alive.

Water climbed up, pushing against the supports, and Reena couldn't help but spy rusted nails that had worked loose. Swallowing hard, she forced herself to cross, making a mental note to tell the park rangers about the decrepit condition. The bridge swayed and she quickened her steps.

"Ashleigh!" Nathan bellowed again, darting toward the red fabric.

By the time she reached his side, he held up a high school raincoat with Vincent's first name stitched above the logo.

Her gut clenched at the abandoned item. Why had—

Rain splattering near a healthy fern contrasted with the rest of the drops landing on the ground. Bending over, she plucked up a clear waterproof bag revealing two cell phones inside.

"Ashleigh's phone." Nathan scraped the tips of his right fingers over the plastic.

The teens had definitely been here, but nothing indicated where they had gone.

Chapter Four

Nathan tightened his fist around the red material. The raincoat flipped up as he turned in a helpless circle, searching for any clue to Ashleigh's whereabouts. Nothing made sense. Why would the teens leave the jacket and their cell phones behind? What would make them become so irresponsible they'd walk away from their lifeline, their only way of communication? Not that the mountains allowed much, if any, signal.

Ashleigh could leave her phone, but not a note or something to help him find her?

Thunder rolled its menace, shaking the ground and mirroring the tempest swirling inside him.

Wind raced through the forest, snatching anything loose in its path. Flinching at the torrent of moisture stinging his exposed cheeks, Nathan forced his wild gaze to focus, then jerked at the white pellets torpedoing toward the earth. Hail. Just peachy. Holes tore through fragile plants while an awful pinging rang over the rocks, joining in nature's discordant symphony.

Movement in Nathan's periphery had him whirling to find Reena ducking, her bare arms covering her head.

Red welts already marred her freckled skin. This had to be ruining Ms. Sunshine's merry world, but his main concern was how Ashleigh was faring. Still, he expected a litany of complaints like his previous girlfriend would hurl at him. *In three, two, one…*

Nothing. Huh. Reena didn't say a word, just hunched her shoulders deeper.

Slightly perplexed, Nathan thrust the jacket toward her. "Put this on." Realizing she probably couldn't hear him, he balanced his foot as best he could on a slick rock protruding between them and wobbled into her space. That subtle scent of strawberries tickled his nose again, now combined with ozone and wet cloth.

Reena jolted and snapped her chin up. Nathan ignored the confusion widening her pupils and draped the raincoat over her shoulders. The backpack made the fit awkward, but she was so small, the material covered enough to keep her protected.

"What about you?" she shouted, fitting the hood over her sopping, bedraggled hair, then jostling the backpack to fit the jacket on correctly.

Angry lines dotted his skin and he winced at the abuse the hail inflicted. "We've got to find the kids." His throat protested the yelling conversation, but he ignored it.

A cold hand clamped on to his forearm, stopping him midturn.

"Did you bring a jacket?"

"We don't have time—"

"Did you?" Reena's grip tightened, cutting off the rant.

Pellets beat into his spine as he dropped his backpack on the rocks and yanked on the zipper, practically tearing it in his haste to open the largest compartment. When his hands felt material, he wrenched it free, a flurry of blue and black waterproof fabric smacking Reena's legs. Seizing the cell phone pouch dangling from Reena's fingers, he stuffed it into his pack, then donned the coat. He hated the delay but begrudgingly knew she was right to force him to wear it. Risking infection burrowing into cuts the hail inflicted just to save a minuscule amount of time was stupid and counterproductive. Score one for the pint-sized youth director, but in his book, she had a massive deficit to overcome just to break even. She'd encouraged the teens to wander the woods alone.

A satisfied glint shone in her hazel eyes, but she remained silent, darting for a break in the foliage leading away from the river. He did his best to follow closely behind. The forest swallowed them whole and the thick canopy along with the black clouds made visibility almost zero.

"It's like night in here," he stated, keeping his gaze glued to the red raincoat.

If Reena responded, he didn't hear it with the noise, but he spied a shiver rocking her body.

Yeah, he agreed with her silent assessment. It was definitely creepy. Or she was just cold and he was the only one spooked. *Very manly, Nathan.* There was a reason he never did much hiking or playing in the woods. Animals wanted to stalk him, trees looked like people closing in, and the terrain wanted to break a bone. But he lived in a mountain town now, so he'd have to come to terms with this new aspect of life sooner or later. He just wished it had been later…much, much later. Financially, Nathan understood why his brother had moved to Bell Edge five years ago. When the job opportunity opened, Scott had to take it, but…there was so much nature and no anonymity.

As Nathan trekked through the mud on something resembling a path, it took him longer than it should have to realize the assault on his body had eased significantly. Hail still fell, but the leaves overhead softened the attack.

"Do you have any idea where you're going?" he bellowed above the shrieking weather raising the hair on his skin for multiple reasons.

Reena's body twisted for a moment, as if to peer over her shoulder, but the hood hid her face. "This way." She pointed ahead.

"That's real helpful," he muttered. *"Ashleigh!"*

Reena jerked and the toe of her boot caught on a patch of leafy vines encroaching over the land. Arms pinwheeling frantically, she worked to catch her balance but overcorrected. Nathan shot his arm out to grab the back of her coat but it snapped out of reach. She flailed to the right and landed in a bush. Leaves and dirt spewed upward while branches twisted at the sudden intrusion.

"Please tell me that's not poison ivy or oak." He hovered beside her legs sprawled in a heap.

A delicate, grimy hand appeared through the foliage and he grasped it to pull her out—

Fiery irises blazed, scorching him in their fury. "You did that on purpose."

"Did what?" He froze midpull at her vehemence. *"You're* the one who tripped. I didn't push you."

Reena tugged on his arm, using him to get her feet back under her. "You yelled loud enough to wake the dead."

"Of course I did." He moved out of striking distance; the inferno hadn't dimmed and he had enough self-preservation to overrule any chivalry demanding he help de-twig her.

"So you admit it." She swiped at the debris clinging to her. The angry motions of her hands would probably leave bruises behind.

"I admit to yelling, not your diving into a bush."

"I didn't *dive*—you know what?" She plucked at a leaf clinging to auburn hair, missing the other four beside it. "Forget it."

Lightning illuminated the oppressive space, highlighting the density of their surroundings. "How in the world are we going to find them?" he asked, not realizing he said the words out loud until they slapped back at him in the wind.

The hazel blaze dimmed to a simmer and the corners of Reena's mouth loosened. "We'll find her," she answered softer, though still above normal speaking level. "Ashleigh's smart and has Vincent, who's loyal to a fault once you earn it. And Vincent couldn't be more devoted to Ashleigh."

Nathan wanted to believe her so much it hurt, but the anvil pressing against his sternum prevented him from internalizing those words. The responsibility of keeping his niece safe threatened to suffocate him. Ashleigh had already lost her mother and father; he could not fail her, too. Shifting his gaze so Reena wouldn't see the anguish sure to be shining bright, Nathan scanned the left side of the "trail," then stilled. "Look." He pointed.

Broken twigs and missing leaves were on either side of a small space between large plants. "I have no tracking skills whatsoever," he continued, "but according to television and movies, it looks like they could've gone that way."

Wet slurping sounded as Reena unlodged her boots from the rivulets of mud and shuffled forward, avoiding the fiendish vines that had landed her in a bush. Straightening from inspecting the breach, she twisted with a grin. "I think you're right."

Chapter Five

Nathan worked hard not to get sucked in by Reena's infectious grin. Nothing about this venture was happy or fun, but he couldn't help puffing with pride at noticing the broken twigs that Reena had missed. Finally, he had contributed something useful.

Reena spread the space between the overgrown shrubs wider and squeezed through, her red jacket a glaring contrast to all the shades of green vegetation.

He followed behind, ignoring the jagged branches digging into his legs and the backs of his hands. Pea-sized hail knocked against his skull in a migraine-inducing beat, adding a fantastic layer—cue sarcasm—of misery to their search.

More plants, vines, and other detritus covered the area, camouflaging any sign of a path. Great. The trunks on the endless trees continued to become thicker the farther away from the river they trekked, reducing the minuscule amount of light and blocking him from seeing much beyond a few feet.

If he couldn't spot the kids, maybe they could hear him. *"Ashleigh!"*

Reena startled and a shrub branch came flying at him. *Whap.* "Hey!" Nathan barked, peeling the leafy limb off his chest.

Twisting, she smirked.

"I *didn't* trip you," he declared, shouting above the increasing winds. "There's no need to assault me."

"Jury's still deliberating on your part," she retorted, turning forward, then raising her voice. "Until we have a verdict, I find you guilty until proven innocent!"

"It's the other way around."

A heavy *crack* echoed a moment before a huge section of a branch broke off, swinging like a pendulum, the kudzu wrapped around the tree preventing the entire piece from hitting the ground.

Slapping a hand to her chest, Reena gulped while Nathan blinked at the monstrosity mere feet to their right. Bushes cushioned the top section but flattened under the weight. That was close. *Too* close. Only the insane would be slogging through a forest right now…or the desperate. Ashleigh was out in this.

Nathan bumped into Reena's backpack, needing her to keep moving.

"You ever see the movie *Crocodile Dundee*?" she asked, eyeing the tops of the trees bowing in the wind ominously.

"You mean the one where Dundee whips out a knife the size of a machete?" Nathan responded, imagining the scene in his mind.

"Exactly!" She handed off branches and trudged forward. "I'm wishing for that monster knife right about now."

He snorted. "I'm thankful it's missing. You'd end up using it on me in some misguided ruling that I've wronged you."

A cackle erupted from her. "Who knew Nathan Porter had a sense of humor?"

"Hey—"

She kept going, cutting off his protest. "There's nothing misguided about my judgment, mister."

"Riiiiiight." Reaching over her shoulder, he snatched at a tangle of vines strangling a copse of shrubs and yanked, clearing enough space for them to squeeze through. "Isn't using a machete a little bloodthirsty for Ms. Sunshine?"

"Depends," she puffed, wiggling between the shrubs that grew against a set of trees.

He swiped the rain out of his eyes as he waited for her to settle on the other side.

She resettled her backpack and turned to him. "Are we talking about using it to clear the vegetation or—"

Too many things happened at once in the next second.

Thunder reverberated, slicing through his eardrums and convulsing the ground.

Nathan staggered just as lightning cracked, exploding in a deafening pitch. Light hurtled toward the earth, sparks flaring across his vision. Pressure hit, pushing him to the side as a massive clap filled the thick air.

One of the trees split in two, like an ax splicing firewood. Heading right toward Reena.

"Reena!" he shouted, not even realizing he'd spoken until his throat protested.

She tossed up her arms, but that did nothing to stop the tree half from slamming into her.

Pain ripped through Reena's palms as a tremendous weight crushed against them, knocking her backward. *Twist!* a booming voice in her brain commanded. Without second guessing, she obeyed, doing everything she could to pivot.

The weight continued to follow her down.

Agony hammered her left side as she landed on it. Her skull bounced against what felt like concrete, twice, as her hip decided to become flush with the earth. Blinking rapidly, trying in vain to make sense of the blob filling her sight, she honed in on tiny cracks etched into... something dark brown... *What?*

Darkness shrouded the blob and with it came peace. Closing her eyes, she sank into the warm black oblivion. So sweet, so—

Vises roughly clamped on her shoulder and biceps, chasing the nirvana away. *Nooo.* She clutched at the void but sharp pain slicing from her hip shattered the remaining serenity.

"—ena!"

Sound invaded like a detonating bomb. Nothing made sense. She longed for the darkness to swallow her whole again.

"Reena," a gruff, male voice barked, knifing through her brain yet helping to lower the overwhelming volume.

Who just spoke? Slitting her eyes, she gazed straight ahead and waited for the blurriness to clear. Tiny cracks on a rough surface captured her attention. Focusing on identifying their meaning helped lessen the pain shooting through different parts of her body.

"Reena," the voice uttered again, the vises tightening, then relaxing.

She knew that voice. Searching her sluggish mind, it came to her. Nathan. Nathan Porter. Ashleigh Porter's mysterious uncle and new guardian.

"Say something," he ordered, high-handedly appointing himself Mr. Bossy Pants.

"Something," she slurred, finding it easier just to do what he said than to fight the daggers puncturing her mind. But in the future she wouldn't allow him to get away with commands.

A hoarse laugh bordering on deranged shook the vises squeezing her. *Vises? What— Oh. Duh.* Those were his hands.

"You hurt?" he asked, shifting. Suddenly the annoying cold pellets stopped hitting her cheek and his face filled her periphery.

"Everywhere." She tilted just enough to see him better; her protesting brain quieted when she found so many emotions flitting through his expressive face, top among them: fear and anxiety. At some point, he had received a scrape against his forehead, the scruff on his jawline had thickened, and mud decorated his skin in a very art nouveau pattern. She'd love to capture him on canvas just like this. Could she portray the inner battle constantly warring inside him? Would he let her?

"Do you like art?" she asked, dazed, her mind already imagining the colors and brushstrokes.

"What?" Alarm and puzzlement overtook a pair of eyes she'd have to use multiple shades of brown and a hint of gold to portray just right.

"I'm an artist," she rambled, her mouth obviously taking over. "Didn't you know that already? I'm sure some of the older ladies at church would've loved to tell you that."

His cheeks pinkened. "I, um, haven't had many conversations at church."

Now that he said it, she remembered him deftly avoiding congregating with anyone.

His gaze studied her face, but he showed nothing of his thoughts this time. "Your being an artist explains a lot, though."

"Hey," she protested a bit too feebly for her liking. "I don't like that tone, mister."

The side of his mouth quirked, then flattened. "It's just you're all about color and imagination. Instead of the tragic creative type, you're in the sunshine and smiles group. Happy, happy, joy, joy and stuff."

"And you're all about being serious and distant." Closing her eyes, she fought against the pain throbbing in her hip.

Nathan remained silent and Mother Nature's chaos filled in. "I'm not always serious," he responded, shocking her blessedly numb. "I play the guitar."

"Really?" Reena cracked her lids and tried to imagine the instrument in his large hands.

"You don't have to sound so shocked," he grumbled over the storm. "I may not think much about art in the terms of paintings and stuff, but I taught myself how to play growing up."

A small slice of peace settled in her chest. He kept everyone at arm's length, yet shared this bit of himself. Needing more time before she had to move, she asked, "You still play?"

He nodded. "My guitar's old and worn, but it still sounds great. Every now and then, I pull it out and strum along to the radio."

"Man," she exhaled as if dismayed. "You really aged yourself there. Don't you know, anyone who's cool digitally streams music now."

"This coming from the woman who hit her head. Your brains are scrambled because I *know* I'm cool as is."

A smile tugged at her lips. "Who knew Mr. Mysterious had jokes?"

"Ha." Pressure squeezed her biceps. "You've lazed around long enough, can you move?"

Lazed? As if. "Let me check." Starting with her toes, Reena worked her way up her body, wiggling and pulsing her muscles and appendages. Her knees stung like a hoard of bees struck, her hips complained *loudly*, her lower back lodged accusations of abuse, her palms weren't speaking to her, and her head squawked way too forcibly. "Nothing feels broken." She hid the litany of suffering competing for attention. They didn't have time for them anyway.

"Thank God." Nathan's shoulders lowered on a long exhale.

"Amen." Steeling herself for a fresh round of pain, she asked, "Can you help me up?"

He jammed his left hand between the muddy ground—which was *not* soft at all—and her arm. With sheer strength, he dragged her backward, brunting her body-weight, then the world spun as she found herself sitting up. *Ohhh. Ouuuuuucccchhhhhh!* Taking shallow breaths, she concentrated on not passing out. *Think of something else. Mind over matter.*

Snapping her gaze off the unsettling drag marks, she froze. "Oh, wow."

Blinking, she could only stare at the new destruction as the storm raged on. Lightning had sliced the trunk of one of the trees into two perfect halves. Those tiny cracks she had studied had been bark...

A tree had almost crushed her.

Unwilling to follow that bone-chilling thought any further, her brain searched for a silver lining.

She could now state with definite authority that yes, a tree *did* make a sound when falling, no matter who was or wasn't in the forest.

Chapter Six

Nathan's heart refused to sink from the middle of his throat. Like a cat, once it reached a certain height, it needed to be rescued.

As his older brother, Scott, used to say after Ashleigh was born, *Ice cold fresh tea!* Sometimes Scott would just exclaim *Fresh tea!* when he was really upset and trying to watch his language around Ashleigh.

Fresh tea. Fresh tea. Fresh tea. A million times. Fresh. Tea.

He had barely comprehended the tremendous sound ripping through the forest let alone had the time to pull Reena out of harm's way. Black spots swarmed the edge of Nathan's vision. He'd never forget the image of Reena crumpled beside the huge trunk. Not moving. Not answering. For eons or, at least, what felt like eons.

His throat choked on a lump. Where was a paramedic when he needed one? If he didn't dislodge his heart soon, he'd suffocate.

A warm gust of air blew his hood off and he wanted to rejoice at the end of the hail. Rain still pounded the earth, but he'd take that over frozen water beating on him like a punching bag.

Reena lifted her face toward the sky, closing her eyes against the precipitation. Mud and dirt covered her skin in interesting ways the rain couldn't seem to wash. Along with the welts from hail and branches fighting back, she resembled a sprite who'd gone into battle with nature and lost. Not that he looked any better. Probably worse.

When she had gazed at him from the ground, he had checked for a concussion. Her pupils looked the same size, but she had definitely seemed out of it. What had brought on the art question? And why did he admit to playing the guitar? The answer immediately jumped into his head. Something deep inside urged him to open up, to share that small piece he rarely told anyone. The vulnerability and pain filling her beautiful hazel eyes called to him, beckoning him to lower his defenses, and hinted that his admission would help ease her misery. For one moment, a sparkle of joy flitted through her face.

Stop. He didn't have time to dwell on the last few moments any longer.

He had a niece to find. And now that he felt sure Reena would survive her battle against Mother Nature, they needed to locate Ashleigh *now*.

The weight of the backpack sapped at his energy, but he heaved his body upward anyway. "I'm going to shout now," he announced, eyeing Reena's still upturned face. *"Ashleigh!"*

Reena's eyelids flew open. "Appreciate the warning this time."

He shrugged while scanning the crowded area for any sign of movement. "Figured I should be nice since you attempted to become a pancake or a walking flashlight."

"And they said chivalry was dead," she responded dryly.

He didn't wait for an invitation, latching on to her wrist resting on her bent knee, he pulled with as much care as he could manage.

"Ahhhhhhgggggggg," she cried. "Where was my warning for *that*?" Two palms flattened on his collarbones and pushed him away, her skin now the pallor of paste.

Allowing his body to step back, he answered, "No time for resting."

Thunder rolled its persistent fury and lightning brightened the sky. He used the illumination to search for a clue.

"Did you see that?" Reena asked, scurrying past him in the same direction they had been traveling before. Albeit with more hobble in her stride than smooth swaying.

"See what?" He hurried to catch up, amazed she wasn't wailing about the agony her muscles had to be in. He wasn't sure if he'd be so silent if the tables were turned. He might have misjudged Ms. Sunshine. This was the second time she had done the exact opposite of what he'd expected. Keeping quiet about the hail was one thing, but having a tree almost crush her? Wow. His level of respect climbed a notch.

Approximately fifteen feet in front of and to the left of the split tree, Reena crouched. Her movements were slow and unsteady, but she managed to pluck something out of the mud and leaves. Standing with obvious effort, pink spots flared on her cheeks and her lips thinned. A slight tremor shook her hand as she opened her fingers and flattened her palm. Abrasions marred her fine-boned hand, some were light scrapes while other cuts seeped blood. Dirt claimed way too much real estate and most likely carried infection.

Hovering his fingers above a particularly wide scrape near her tiny wrist, he murmured, "We need to clean these and put on salve."

"As soon as we find the kids," she responded, shifting her palm from beneath his hand. "Look at what I found."

Refocusing his attention, he stared at the item about the size of a thumbnail. The rain began washing it clean, steadily revealing more silver metal. His stomach dropped, then soared.

"We're on the right track," he crowed, barely refraining from grabbing the charm and running, screaming his niece's name.

"It's Ashleigh's, right?" Reena asked, closing her fingers around the metal.

"I'm sure of it." He faced the opening he could now see torn into the vegetation. "Her father gave her a charm for her bracelet every year on her birthday. It's always something that commemorated the past year." Leading the way, he plunged through the bushes and yelled over his shoulder, "Ashleigh never failed to text me a picture." A pang tore through his heart. This year Scott couldn't give her a charm. Should he continue the tradition or would that be intruding on something special she'd had with her dad? Doubts plagued him and he longed for his brother's advice.

"Which year was this charm?" Reena's question kept the helplessness and anger at the senseless death at bay.

Studying the ground for another clue, he mentally flipped through the birthdays. "I think it was three years ago. She took some type of home and family class in school. You know, where they have to cook, and sew, and stuff?"

Reena began laughing. The musical sound flitted over the harsh storm, calming the dissonance inside him.

"Oh, I remember!" Reena took the spread of shrub branches from him. "She wanted extra credit, so she found a pattern for a pair of sweatpants instead of the pillow everyone else was making."

Vivid memories of Ashleigh and Scott's phone call replayed in his head and he softly chuckled. "It was a disaster."

"The youth group talked about it for weeks." Reena snorted. "One pant leg was four inches shorter than the other—"

"And somehow she sewed the middle shut, so she couldn't put them on," he finished.

After the laughter died, Reena asked, "So your brother decided to give her a sewing machine charm?"

Nathan shook his head at the sudden grief trying to get a foothold. "Scott was always ready for a joke or a prank, and you have to admit, those pants were pretty memorable."

"I'd say."

He couldn't talk about it anymore. He just…couldn't. *"Ashleigh!"*

Wait. Nathan halted, not daring to breathe. Straining to listen over the wind and thunder, he wondered if his mind was playing tricks on him.

Reena stopped beside him, cocking her head. After a moment, she bellowed, *"Vincent!"* Torment flashed and she clutched her temples, massaging them in slow circles. "Remind me not to do that again."

Pity rose, fighting with the urgency. "Cover your ears." Once she had her thumbs in place, he roared, *"Ashleigh!"*

It wasn't much, but he swore he heard a higher-pitched tone on the wind.

Chapter Seven

Barreling through the plants like a steamroller, Nathan slapped at branches and vines blocking his way.

"Ashleigh!" Not slowing to listen for a reply, he continued.

Birds and animals hurled irate comments as he passed, probably about him barging through their territory. He didn't care.

Cut left. Swerve right. Almost pivot. The trees became a macabre slalom course, defying him to conquer it. Challenge accepted. He'd allow nothing less than triumph.

"Nathan!" Reena's voice was somewhere too far behind him.

"I can't wait," he shouted, plowing ahead. "I hear her."

Left, right, sharp right, left—

Ugh. Stupid vine. He swiped at the stems assaulting his nose and right eye and spat out the fat leaves.

One second he was angling to avoid a very robust trunk, the next he was staring up at the branches of that same tree. From the wrong angle. Air escaped his lungs as a sharp burn sliced up his spine. It took two tries to inflate his lungs. The wheeze emanating from his throat sounded anything but masculine. Slapping a palm on the ground, he pushed. It slipped out from under him and he landed on his back. Again.

The burn near his spine sharpened. *Ugh.* Using only abdominal muscles for the second attempt, he successfully sat up, his spine twinging in the process. Gently twisting, he glared at a stone mostly buried in the mud. "Thanks a lot," he muttered to it, rubbing the aching spot near his liver.

As sudden as the temperature dropped earlier, heat now swamped the forest, adding another level of misery.

"You can't run like that," Reena panted, jogging into view. "Leaves act like ice when they're wet."

"No kidding," he grumped, embarrassment heating his cheeks and deflating what remained of his ego.

She offered a hand to help him up, but he scowled at it. "Reena, don't take this wrong way, but I'm *not* accepting your assistance."

Her chin snapped back and she dropped her hand, her eyebrows lowering in confusion.

"I have to weigh, like, twice as much as you." He blinked at the constant water in his face. "Your palms are a mess and your sore muscles are probably screaming. There's no way I'm going to be a total jerk and yank on your arm to stand."

Carefully gaining his feet, he ground his teeth at his T-shirt and shorts clinging to his back and legs awkwardly. Mud encased him from head to toe.

"You've got…" Reena reached up and plucked a twig with two odd-looking green leaves out of his hair.

Awesome. "I don't think any amount of rain is going to clean me up." He stretched tall to loosen the muscles protesting the stone's punch and scanned the surroundings. *"Ashleigh!"*

Thunder drowned a potential response.

"Come on." Nathan began running again, but this time he dialed back the recklessness to just "urgent" level.

"Uncle Nathan." A faint female voice echoed from somewhere on his right.

"Ashleigh!" Adjusting as best he could with the rough terrain, his soul burst with elation. "I'm coming!"

Like a weird game of Marco Polo, every time Nathan called his niece's name, she answered with his, guiding him ever closer. The rain insisted on falling in sheets thick enough to cut visibility and made the whole venture as miserable as possible. After what felt like an hour, but was probably a few minutes, he finally spied a thin arm waving frantically in the air.

"Ashleigh," Nathan cried, darting toward her.

"Uncle Nathan," she answered, then disappeared.

"Hey!" Alarm iced his veins. "Ashleigh!"

"I'm fine." A muffled response carried to him.

Two seconds later, the top half of her popped into view, shooting up like a human rocket. Fern leaves and other plants blocked the rest of her, frustrating him to no end. He had to know she wasn't hurt. Had to see with his own eyes she was okay.

Trampling through the forest like elephants, he and Ashleigh stomped toward each other, unheeding of what was in their way. Behind her, he spied Vincent, almost a half foot taller, following in her wake, but Nathan didn't pay attention beyond that. Finally breaking into a clearing, he spread his arms wide and Ashleigh jumped, slamming into him with her entire body. Elation made his brain dizzy or maybe it was his feet dancing them in circles. Squeezing her tighter, he laughed at the squeal deafening his left eardrum.

"You are so gross!" she exclaimed, pulling her upper half back and glowering at the muck coating parts of her skin. "Did you *roll* in the mud?"

And just like that, fury blazed through his veins.

"Fresh tea, Ashleigh Porter," Nathan barked. A garbled choke sounded behind him. Unpeeling his niece, he set her back down. "What were you thinking?"

Color drained from Ashleigh's face, but her chin jutted. Experience told him she was digging in for a fight. Wonderful. Hopefully her foolish decision was based in guilt she hoped to bluff through and not some deep-seated need to act out because he had taken the place of her father. Oy. He was so not qualified for this, but it was his duty now and he'd do his best.

"Uh," Vincent stammered, bravely moving to Ashleigh's side, "Mr. Porter—"

"Not now," Nathan responded, not breaking eye contact with his fifteen-year-old gray-hair maker.

"Vincent." Reena, the self-appointed diplomat, intervened. "Let's give them a minute."

But the teen didn't budge. He crossed his arms and produced the same mulish body language as Ashleigh.

Whatever. Vincent could have it his way. Slowly and very obviously, Nathan studied his niece from head to toe, then did the same with Vincent. Ashleigh squirmed, caught herself, stopped, then wiggled a bit again under his weighted gaze. Vincent's spine snapped straight, red dotted his cheeks, and his hands balled into fists, but he remained unmoving otherwise. Both looked like drowned rats and mud stained their clothes, but nothing was torn or ripped. Just a few minor scratches dotted their skin.

Overall, they both appeared healthy. *Thank you, Lord.* The prayer popped into his head and he allowed it even though he wasn't really speaking to God at the moment. Seeing her healthy and whole allowed him to breathe easier and think clearer.

Thunder cracked, then rolled in intensity, adding its thoughts to the moment.

"You scared me half to death." Nathan's finger jabbed toward his niece in accusation. "I thought something horrible happened to you."

Guilt or maybe surprise flashed in Ashleigh's brown eyes. "I—"

"I kept imagining you had broken a leg or got trapped between rocks," he barreled over her, his fears refusing to stay bottled. "Or something equally terrifying that stopped you from returning on time."

"We're fine." Vincent swiped his face, but it didn't stop the water from wetting it again.

"Yes." Nathan lasered his gaze to the teen, then re-settled on Ashleigh. "I can see that."

Ashleigh winced. "Uncle Nathan—"

"Don't 'Uncle Nathan' me in that placating tone," he growled. "Why are you two *here* and not with the rest of the group?"

A look passed between Ashleigh and Vincent that Nathan couldn't decipher. His anger relit its fuse.

"Don't even *think* about lying to me." His finger had a mind of its own, continuously jabbing and pointing at the teens.

"We all decided to split the list," Ashleigh explained, twisting and smoothing the bottom of her T-shirt.

"You promised me you'd stay with your team," Nathan countered, surprised at how the deceit hurt. She hadn't robbed a bank or snorted drugs, but she had broken a promise…albeit a small one, but his heart panged all the same.

"I know but," Ashleigh rushed to say, making it sound like *iknowbut*, "we figured we could finish it faster and have time for a swim."

"That still doesn't explain why you're here or why Rachel and Andy couldn't find you." Lightning brightened the sky, lifting the dark oppression for a few seconds. "Where did you go? What were you two doing?" More scenarios invaded Nathan's mind. Panic swirled with the anger and he swallowed against the latest bombshell—

"Uncle Nathan," Ashleigh retorted in that scandalized/offended/mocking tone teenagers had perfected. "We weren't doing *anything*."

"I swear, Mr. Porter," Vincent chimed in, his shoulders rammed back. "We just wanted to cool off in the river."

Relief coursed through Nathan. No latest bombshell. Black spots dotted his vision and he had to inhale before he passed out. Truth rang through their words, convincing him they really had been swimming and nothing more.

He had to have aged a hundred years in the last thirty seconds. "Okay, but this is a far cry from the meeting space *and* where we found your jacket and cell phones."

Ashleigh bit her bottom lip while Vincent stiffened.

"There's no signal—"

"You think that makes it okay?" Nathan cut Vincent's explanation off. "It's not. If you had to move from this spot, you could have gotten a signal in your new location. You never abandon a potential lifeline."

Ashleigh twisted the hem again. "But nothing bad happened."

Nathan studied the canopy to calm himself. The teens didn't know. Didn't understand.

"Something bad *did* happen," he stated coolly, focusing his attention on Reena. Her face bore a mixture of resignation and anxiousness. "Did you know Reena was almost struck by lightning?"

"What?" Ashleigh and Vincent asked at the same time his niece's hand flew to the bottom of her throat while Vincent rocked back on his heels.

"Nath—"

"It missed." He spoke over Reena's warning tone. "But she was almost crushed by a tree instead. A. Tree. She literally risked her life to search for you two in this storm."

"That's enough." Reena parked herself in front of him. "I'm fine. Give them a chance to explain."

Nathan opened his mouth to argue her assessment but Reena's glare had him crossing his arms instead. Planting his boots shoulder-width apart, he deadpanned, "I can't wait to hear it."

"We—"

"No." Nathan shook his head at Vincent. "I want to hear it from *you*." He pointed at his niece, needing her to speak. To force her to own her actions, to account for them and not hide behind someone else's explanation. His mother taught him that lesson growing up and it worked—much to his chagrin.

Ashleigh shifted and worried the bottom of her shirt. "There's not much more to tell," she began. "The team split up. Vincent and I finished, so we jumped in the river to cool off." She visibly inhaled. "The current was really strong and it scared me. I couldn't keep my feet under me, so Vincent helped me to the riverbank. We were farther down than we realized, but before we could get oriented and walk back to our stuff, the storm hit."

A vivid image sprang in his mind. He blanched and swayed at the sudden blood loss in his brain. She could have drowned or been swept away...

Ashleigh's shoulders slumped and her gaze fixed on a bush to the right of him. "We could barely see a thing in the rain, so we ran, looking for cover from the lightning." She motioned to something behind her. "We found a space big enough to hide in beneath some fallen trees and plants."

Nathan dug his fingernails into his palms to clear the mental video.

Reena gently bumped his biceps with her shoulder. He took solace in the connection. How she knew he needed the touch, he didn't know, nor did he really care. It helped.

Leaning closer to Reena, he faced his niece. "You almost drowned..." Nathan couldn't go on. "Fresh tea, Ashleigh. I can't even..." A tremor started in his toes, rising steadily to his head. "I just..." He tried again, but couldn't force the words out. "I can't lose you, too." In two steps, he closed the distance and wrapped his niece in his arms.

Chapter Eight

The lump in Reena's throat made swallowing almost impossible. The strengthening bond between Nathan and Ashleigh was amazing. Over the last six months, Reena had witnessed the two grow from friendly relatives to this…this incredible moment. Anyone else might not have noticed the change, but Reena had. From the first day Nathan Porter had walked into church, so uncomfortable and awkward, he had piqued her interest. It made no sense. He didn't encourage conversation and threw out vibes to be left alone. But she watched him from afar anyway, drawn like a brush to a canvas. Before this trip, they had spoken less than a hundred words, and earlier today, their exchanges were not stellar, yet she continued to be fascinated.

At the emotional display, Vincent studied his stained boots with supreme concentration.

Nathan could have handled the conversation better, but she understood. After hearing Ashleigh's explanation, Reena wanted to yell, too. She could have lost both teens… *Dear Lord, thank you for saving them*.

Shying away from the morbid path, she redirected her

thoughts. If she had to guess, she knew exactly whose idea it had been to swim. Vincent had such a crush on Ashleigh—one he didn't realize Reena knew about—he'd follow the girl just about anywhere and allow himself to be talked into just about anything short of illegal. That didn't make Ashleigh a bad person. In fact, she was a typical teen when it came to decision-making; thinking mostly in the present instead of the potential repercussions. But that meant Reena couldn't truly rely on Vincent to have sound judgment around Ashleigh, either, when in every other instance the boy thought and acted like a sixty-year-old.

Kind of like how Reena felt right now. *Ugh.*

Ashleigh and Nathan needed more time, but they didn't have it.

Though she was loathe to intrude on the moment, Reena announced, "We should head back." Every cell she owned begged her to crawl into the shelter the kids had found and rest, not start traveling again.

Nathan untangled from Ashleigh. His physique dwarfed both Reena and his niece, but she had never felt intimidated. He might be standoffish—with a surprising sense of humor—but a bully never jibed.

Wiggling her backpack off her shoulders—*oh, dear Lord, help me.* Fire burned through her muscles, demanding she stop moving, but she couldn't take the weight another second. "The rest of the church group is waiting in the van." Reena soldiered on, dropping the pack near her feet. Mud splashed over her boots, but she could care less. So what if her tent strapped to the bottom became filthy. She'd be in her own comfy bed tonight. "We need to join them."

No one moved. Ashleigh gnawed on her lip, hope

brimming beside the drying tears in her eyes, most likely anticipating being forgiven. Vincent divided his focus between his boots, then Ashleigh, then Nathan, then the boots again. And Nathan's spine had loosened but his expression still bore traces of anxiety, horror, and a telltale red rim that showed a few tears had escaped.

Oh boy. "Excellent idea, Reena," she answered herself with false exuberance. "It's dangerous to stay out in the storm."

That got a reaction from Nathan. He scrubbed a large hand over his grimy face, then grimaced, his lip curling at his streaked palm. "We'll talk about this again later." His narrowing gaze promised the conversation wouldn't be pleasant.

Ashleigh nodded, her hope draining.

The senior Porter unzipped his jacket, then managed to wiggle out of it with his backpack still on.

Impressive.

"Take this." He offered the waterproof coat to his niece.

Like a lightbulb clicking on, Reena realized she still had on Vincent's jacket. The poor guy was soaked to the bone and she wore his only defense. *Way to be on the ball, Reena.* She blamed the headache and hip pain for the oversight. "Vincent." She began peeling off the red slicker. "I'm so sorry. Take your coat back."

"No." The teen jammed his hands into his raggedy shorts' pockets. "You keep it on."

"I'll be fine." She waggled it. "I've got one in my pack."

"Oh. Okay." He took the high school jacket, glanced at Ashleigh as she squirmed into Nathan's, then put his on. The drenched fabric molded to his body, but it had to be better than water continuously saturating his clothing and hair.

In less than a second, the hem of Reena's T-shirt dripped with water, the rain waterlogging it completely. A hank of her hair plastered against her cheek, blocking part of her sight...were those leaves sticking to the strands? Fantastic. The rest of her shoulder-length locks were like free weights pulling on her skull.

"Reena." Nathan's voice stopped her from bending toward her pack. "We need to clean your hands."

Vincent's chin snapped up and he pushed closer, catching one of her arms she tried to hide behind her back. "Reena." The teen's brows drew down. "They're red and some cuts are still bleeding," he accused, his thumb digging into her wrist vein, then releasing.

"Psh." She downplayed. "There's barely any blood."

The flat expressions on both Vincent and Nathan's faces said they didn't buy her evaluation.

"They could be infected," Vincent declared.

Nathan nodded.

Two oversized males ganging up on her sucked all the air from the space. No matter how well-meaning, she didn't want her injuries analyzed and diagnosed.

She tugged her arm free and swished it dismissively. Neither realized her hips and head hurt a thousand times worse than her palms. "We'll address them when we get back to the van. We shouldn't be in the forest any longer than we have to."

Nathan opened his mouth but Reena glowered him into silence. Yes, she had told him she'd deal with it when they found the kids, but it didn't feel right to take the time to bandage herself. The urgency to escape the storm and rejoin the church group drove her now, setting the priorities—

Lightning! her mind cried at a flash of bright yellow in

her periphery. Jumping back without thinking, she threw
her hands up and swallowed against the adrenaline raging in her veins. When nothing shook or sparked, she
lowered her arms, and blinked. Her sight latched on to
the yellow and she wished the ground would swallow her
whole. Could she be any more of a dork? Vincent gaped
at her with his jaw open and eyes wide. In his raised fist,
he brandished her raincoat. Her bright *yellow* raincoat.
Not lightning. Clothing. She had jumped out of an evil
raincoat's path.

"Don't mind me," she uttered weakly, adding an idi-
otic chuckle that shook in time with her trembling body.
Adrenaline still ruled, making her queasy and her head
ache harder. Because, apparently, she needed more suffering.

"Um," Nathan began.

"Not a word," she commanded, pointing at his chest.
"I'm fine. Just got spooked by my stupid coat, okay?"

"Suurre." Nathan's eyebrows furrowed. "I mean, I'll
admit it *is* bright, but I'm not sure your jacket's worth
breaking the high jump record." He motioned to the near-
est tree. "You did earn extra points for trying to clear that
branch up there, though."

"Still got jokes." Reena appreciated his attempt at levity. She obviously had a few issues to work through.

Offering Nathan a grateful smile, she gently slid the
coat from Vincent's fingers.

The teen snapped his mouth closed audibly. "I didn't
mean to scare you. I—"

"Vincent." She patted his forearm. "You didn't do anything wrong. Thanks for pulling this out for me." As she
donned the coat, she silently blasted her injuries, making
up declarations when her usual litany ran dry. As much as

she tried to school her face, by Nathan's pinched expression, he saw everything she wanted to hide. Excellent. *Note to self. Add "extremely observant" to Nathan's list of characteristics.* Hopefully she'd at least fooled Vincent and Ashleigh. The teens needed her to be strong, not a burden. They depended on her to lead them off the mountain safely and be their rock during a literal storm. Just because she wished she had a rock of her own right now didn't do a bit of good. She'd bite the bullet and act like a church teen director, not a lightning victim. Er, starting now.

As usual when she felt stressed, she searched for a silver lining. Having wet clothes stuck to her body wasn't ideal, but the uncomfortable sensation did have one positive: it helped combat the thick humidity brought on by the storm.

"Ready, Madam Director?" Nathan asked, dipping his chin as if bowing.

"I like the respect." She grinned even though he was being sarcastic.

He shook his head but she spied his lips twitching. "Of course you do." Stepping closer, he uttered in a low tone, "Seriously, though. Are you okay to make the trip back?"

Touched at his thoughtfulness, a tight cord inside loosened. "Thanks." Her fingers grazed his forearm in appreciation of his concern. "We really do need get to the van as soon as possible," she replied to distract him from realizing she hadn't answered his question. She refused to lie, and the truth would only make him feel worse when they could do nothing about her injuries.

"Then we'll follow you."

Vincent hoisted her pack onto his back and Reena had no energy to fight him for it.

"Thanks, Vincent."

The sight of the smile replacing the shock nestled into the special place in her heart with his name on it. His mother had done one heck of a job raising the young man on her own, and Reena reveled in watching him grow into adulthood.

Forging the path back was much easier since she and Nathan had left gaping breaks and obvious marks of where they had traveled.

When she arrived in a small clearing, Reena's feet halted, refusing to take another step.

"Ice cold fresh tea," Ashleigh exclaimed. Her uncle broke through the foliage and stopped close to his niece, then shot daggers at the sight before them.

Reena's stomach plummeted and her heart raced like a locomotive. The tree that had tried to crush her looked even worse than she remembered. Jagged spikes of wood shot up from the exposed center while two halves of a once healthy trunk bowed toward the ground, touching in some places. *Thank you, Lord*, she prayed, inhaling against the cold in her veins. Normally, she'd enjoy the sensation battling the muggy heat, but not in this instance.

Ashleigh dropped the hand covering her mouth and gawked at Reena. She blinked twice, her enlarged pupils appearing almost cartoonish, then threw her arms around her uncle, burying her face in his chest. "I'm sorry," she muffled into the cloth and dirt.

His tanned arms wrapped her tight and he placed his cheek on top of her head. "I know you are, sweetheart. Now do you understand why I'm acting like a lunatic? I kept imagining this scenario and worse happening to you."

She nodded, her face smearing the mud. "Yes, and I *swear* I'll never do something like this again."

"That, I believe." Nathan tore his gaze off the mangled trunk to focus on Reena. From the glint sparking in his eyes, he had to be replaying the lightning striking and her going down with the tree.

She shuddered—

"I'm sorry, too, Reena."

She snapped her attention to the tall teen towering beside her.

Vincent's shoulders rounded and he couldn't seem to look away from the split trunk. "I know I disappointed you." His breath hitched. "And I hate that."

Reena carefully wrapped an arm around the young man only an inch or so shorter than Nathan. Her muscles protested the side hug, but she told them to stuff it. "I may be disappointed and we *are* going to talk about the decisions you both made, count on that…"

Vincent grimaced but nodded as if not surprised another lecture loomed on the horizon.

"…but I forgive you." She squeezed him tighter. "I'm beyond relieved you two are okay."

Vincent remained stiff and unyielding.

"Hey, you and I are fine," she soothed, knowing why he was beating himself up so hard. "You're still my favorite teenager in the whole world, but only as long as you don't tell anyone else and get me in trouble."

The left side of Vincent's mouth lifted and he ducked his head, his spine finally relaxing. She held in a chuckle at the pink blossoming on this strong guy's ears.

Thunder crackled, signaling it was time to go. She hightailed it as fast as her aching hips allowed. Speed level: Limping Turtle.

Chapter Nine

Bringing up the rear of the bedraggled group, Nathan made sure no one fell behind or needed help. It felt odd not being in charge. He owned his own company and employed a staff, but in this instance, he had no problem being the caboose. Beyond a construction site or taking care of his own yard, he had no experience with nature, let alone becoming this expedition's leader. Not that Reena should be in that role right now, either. A gust of wind could blow her beaten frame over. If her gait skewed any more in her wince-worthy hobble, she'd become permanently disfigured.

His boot landed in the thousandth puddle, spraying mud up his calves. *Urg.* At this point, the environment had claimed every inch of his skin. Dirt ran down his arms in channels and mud streamed from his hair down his spine. So pleasant.

Ashleigh stole another look at him, this time in the guise of observing a bird flap to another branch. Since they had left the downed tree, she had been watching him. Studying him like a science project she feared she'd failed. She had. Failed spectacularly, but he had pretty much forgiven her.

"You okay?"

Nathan snapped his gaze off a bush of white and pink flowers bowing beneath the rain to find Reena planted in front of him. "Where did you come from?" he blurted, rattled he hadn't sensed her.

"Um." She thumbed over her shoulder. "That way."

"Cute." He peered beyond her to find Ashleigh and Vincent waiting near a set of trees with fungus growing on the bark like spiraling steps.

She pretended to curtsy, grimacing at the action. "You look like your mind's racing. Want to talk about it?"

Did he? "Shouldn't we keep moving?"

"We can walk and talk at the same time," she replied, turning to face forward. "I'm talented like that."

He couldn't get over her disposition. She had been hit by a tree, drenched by the rain, and trekked after wayward teens, yet still had the ability to remain positive. No wonder people gravitated toward her, himself included, much to his frustration. But did he want to talk? He hated analyzing feelings and opening up meant letting another person into his life. His capacity was maxed out.

Talk, Nathan, his inner voice commanded. *You need it.* He did, and somehow Reena didn't make him feel stupid or awkward for wrestling with everything that had happened. The other church attendees were friendly, but he never felt comfortable or motivated to befriend anyone, and yet, as he gazed upon Ms. Sunshine, a surge of conflicting emotions rose to the forefront.

"Hey," she stated softly, lifting her arm but stopping short of touching his. "You don't have to—"

"I can't get the image of Ashleigh almost drowning

out of my mind." The words tumbled out of his mouth of their own volition.

Reena nodded, her skin losing a bit of color. "Me, too. We could have lost them both."

His shoulders relaxed. She hadn't laughed or lectured him. He could do this. Resuming the walk, he and Reena passed the teens. "Hang back, but not out of sight, okay?" he instructed, not wanting to be overheard.

"Okay," Ashleigh answered, studying one of the fungi she'd plucked off a trunk.

Waiting until the teens began following at a comfortable distance, he kept going. "I believe she understands she scared me and accepts her decision to go swimming was the wrong one." He scraped the hair on his chin. "I just have trouble swallowing the fact that her desire to go for a swim had overridden common sense."

"I feel the same way." Reena increased the pace a notch. "Vincent knows better. On previous outings, I *taught* him to assess the current before wading in, yet they got caught by surprise."

Slapping at the leaves on a low-jutting branch, he wished the imagery playing through his mind would falter as easily as the vegetation. But no, just like the leaves smacking him in the back of the head, imagining losing Ashleigh decked him, too.

He shook his head, water flinging in both directions. "She couldn't wait for this trip."

"Yeah." Reena exhaled, and a small smile lifted her lips. "She was so excited when I announced the camping weekend."

"I thought we might enjoy a little adventure together." Nathan eased a set of branches back. "Hike a few trails, tell some stories around a campfire, eat too many s'mores…" He trailed off, wrangling his thoughts back in line. "I figured if I was here, I could protect her." He snorted derisively. "Look how well that's turned out."

"She's safe." Reena bumped his shoulder. "She and Vincent were typical teenagers who had God looking out for them. With divine intervention, they remained unharmed."

"Yeah." Nathan grimaced at the sour taste filling his mouth. "God has been so *benevolent* to the Porters lately." His fingers curled into fists and he jammed them into his pockets, fighting the rising anger.

"He has."

Nathan ripped his gaze off the trail ahead and gawked at Reena. "Are you serious?"

She held up her hands as if to ward off the fury making him tremble. "I'm not saying it's okay that Scott died. Far from it, but God's given you to Ashleigh, and her to you." Her arms dropped and they resumed walking. "You'll heal each other and, in the meantime, you've both got me whenever you need it."

He swallowed against harsh words bursting to break free. He didn't want platitudes and pretty philosophies. He wanted his brother back. He wanted Ashleigh to have her father. And he wanted to finally feel like he knew what he was doing again.

"Can you do me a favor?"

He lifted his head. He already regretted opening his mouth, now she wanted him to do something? "Depends," he managed to utter without barking.

She smiled, though it didn't reach her eyes. "Will you take a peek at the teens behind us? Really look at Ashleigh."

Not seeing a reason to say no, he did as asked. He saw

the two walking side by side, as closely as he was with Reena. Vincent was explaining something, the words too low for Nathan to hear, while Ashleigh nodded. Then her arm hooked around Vincent's elbow and she leaned her head on his biceps.

Nathan turned around.

Reena winced as she stepped over a sodden log. "Ashleigh is healthy. Granted, she's still grieving for her dad, and will for the rest of her life, but she's not crushed under the weight of it." The pressure of her hand on his forearm forced him to listen to her words. "Nathan, she's *strong*. Your niece was able to attend this weekend trip because she's had *you* by her side."

Right, he started to scoff, but something inside him wouldn't let him get away with ignoring Reena's observation. Ashleigh was the only person who mattered. Not his litany of wants…and…he couldn't argue with Reena's assessment. The revelation dawned. Today alone, he'd heard his niece freely laugh, joke, and talk to her friends. She participated in all the activities… "Ms. Sunshine…" He had no idea how to finish the sentence.

"Bask in my warming rays," she quipped, intuiting he needed a break from the heavy topic. She tossed him a full smile.

His heart skipped at the unfiltered radiance beaming at him. Uh, wow. He released the resentment and doubt he'd been harboring, and felt lighter. Not totally free, but he could finally take a deep breath and not choke on it.

Chuckling at Reena's obscenely yellow coat, he couldn't imagine her choosing any other color. It just screamed bright happiness in the face of nature's soggy gloom. So her.

He stepped into another puddle. By this point, he'd be lucky to find solid ground—

And then he heard it. In the distance. The roar of the river. They were almost to the bridge.

Falling into a comfortable silence, Nathan contemplated Ashleigh's companion, Vincent. The sixteen-year-old was almost as tall as Nathan and had a bit of muscle to his frame. The calluses Nathan had spied earlier told him the kid wasn't afraid of hard work, which Nathan respected. Ashleigh lit up every time Vincent neared and, if his instincts were right, Vincent had just as big a crush on his niece. While not surprising, it brought up another hard issue he had no clue how to handle. Had Scott already had The Talk with her? *Ugh.* A shudder rippled through him. Wishing for a bottle of brain bleach to kill *all* traces of that thought, Nathan resolutely moved on. He'd just have to watch them closely. He didn't know Vincent well, but he liked the teen. The small interactions he'd had at church and this weekend showed the boy to be serious with a stable moral compass. Ashleigh had mentioned an after-school job, and Nathan admired the teen for learning to balance life, school, and work. Add the fact that Vincent and Ashleigh both loved attending church and had friends in the youth group, and Nathan had hope. Unlike his own upbringing, the teens had a strong foundation to control the raging hormones plaguing their bodies. A good thing since he intended to see Ashleigh graduate college and rule the world.

Rushing water reverberated louder.

The tree density grew sparse and the widths of the trunks became progressively thinner. Hallelujah.

His quota of panic and fear had been met for the *year.* Maybe even spreading into the decade's allotment.

Plunging through the final obstacle, Nathan paused beside the river. Reena, Ashleigh, and Vincent stopped a foot from the bank...or the area the bank now claimed. Wow, the water had risen. Pieces of ferns reached through the surface as if begging to be rescued. The river crashed into protruding rocks as white foam rushed past in a frenzy, its journey like a roller-coaster ride.

The roar of the water muted everything else, even the fierce storm overhead.

Reena moved toward the bridge. Dread squeezed his abdomen and his boots felt like twenty pounds of cement.

Water smashed against the supports, the fatigued wood deteriorating by the second. When he had crossed it the first time, he had only been thinking of finding Ashleigh. Now he wasn't sure if the decrepit thing would hold petite Reena, let alone Vincent and himself.

Groaning rumbled a sickly warning. An ominous pause ensued, then part of the bridge tilted, the surface now at a twenty-degree angle.

Nathan's arm shot out to stop Reena from taking another step, but he got a fistful of air. She had jumped back, landing at the edge of a dark green bush.

At the same time Nathan lunged for Reena, Vincent yanked Ashleigh against him, her back to his chest. Excellent reflexes, and Nathan appreciated that the teen's first reaction was to protect Ashleigh and not himself.

Nathan maneuvered toward Reena. The chalky skin of her face greeting him when she glanced his way, then back at the bridge did nothing to quell the anxious fear grabbing hold.

"We can't cross that," he announced, not knowing what else to say.

As if the structure agreed, a horrific screech rent the

air. Another section of the bridge twisted, slats of wood shot upward, then dropped into the water. On the other side, support pylons ripped out of the ground, splashing into the rapids. The water latched on to the offering and dragged it away, smashing pieces against the rocks. Unable to withstand the momentum, the rest of the bridge's top tore loose with an awful wail and plunged beneath the water. Jagged and decimated, the bit of wood remaining might be large enough for a bird to land on, but didn't do them any good.

"That was our way back to the van," Reena declared, causing Nathan's heart to climb back into his throat.

Chapter Ten

Reena gawked at the bridge steadily disappearing out of sight. Thunderous bangs silenced the forest every time wood shattered against the protruding rocks.

Their access across the river now surfed the rapids like a convict escaping prison, relentlessly gaining as much distance from its jailer as possible. Debris and a few supports were the only visuals left of the long-standing structure.

"What did you say?" Ashleigh asked, horror lacing her voice.

No matter how hard Reena tried, she couldn't force her gaze from the river. An insane part of her hoped the bridge would come back. Either that or she'd wake up from this bizarre nightmare and find herself in her apartment over her art gallery—

"Reena."

Nathan's deep voice ripped her from hoping. She wasn't dreaming. And she wasn't in her apartment. No. She stood beside a river in a thunderstorm with pain dogging every breath and rain drowning every inch.

A firm grip encircled her forearm. "Hey."

Following the strong fingers up to their owner's face, she found Nathan studying her. Water streamed off his nose and filtered along his scruff. Wind pulled at his hair, riffling the few pieces not coated in mud, and his irises… Oh. The surreal fog fell from her mind. His gaze seemed one step away from panic.

"Nathan." She divided her attention between the missing bridge and the man who intrigued her more and more with his unfolding depths. The man who enticed her curiosity to uncover his mysteries. "That was our only way across."

His pupils expanded.

"What?" Ashleigh cried, tearing loose from Vincent. "You can't be serious."

"Please tell me you're just kidding." Nathan's skin leached into the color of milk.

Ashleigh hugged herself, leaning into Vincent's grip on her shoulder.

Reena rubbed her roiling stomach, then stopped the telling action. She had to pretend everything would be fine. The teens didn't need to be freaked out any more than they were. Attempting a grin, she mimed her next words. "I should pull out my trusty engineer hat and whip up a new bridge like MacGyver."

"There's got to be another way across," Vincent protested.

"Does Ms. Sunshine have MacGyver's talent?" Nathan asked, blessedly picking up on her effort to diffuse the situation. "I'd pay to see it."

"Aren't *you* a contractor?" Reena pointed at his chest, continuing the folly. "Bet you could slap something together."

"Oh, sure," Nathan answered, his head bobbing a little

too much to be believable. "I'd be all kinds of help. My electrical engineer skills will come in so handy right now. If you want me to figure out how to hot-wire a tree or—"

A bark of laughter burst out of Reena.

Nathan's lips twitched.

Unable to stop the torrent, she let the laughter take over. Expressions ranging from "Huh?" to smiling but unsure why, beamed at her.

Waving a hand in front of her face, she tried to catch her breath. "I'm sorry," she wheezed, unable to stop. Holding her stomach, she bent and roared with more laughter.

"It's—" she tried to speak again "—just…" Tears flowed from her eyes. "Hot…wire…a…tree!" Losing it again, she leaned on her abused knee.

A few snickers joined her then those grew into full-belly laughter in moments. She wasn't sure who was holding up whom, but no one could stand straight.

"Anyone else seeing cartoonish trees," Vincent wheezed, "with a bunch of wires in their branches, zooming through the forest on their roots?"

"Yes!" Ashleigh spread her arms above her head and imitated a turbo tree by hustling along the bank, then returning to stand beside Vincent.

"Fresh tea." Nathan swiped his watering eyes. "I really needed that."

Reena's tenuous hold on her laughter started to crack. "What is it with you and fresh tea? You love it? You hate it? What?"

"It's my dad's saying," Ashleigh answered, wiping her nose along her jacket's sleeve. "He tried not to curse around me so he was forever saying, 'Ice cold fresh tea.'"

Her smile wobbled. "When he's…" She cleared her throat. "When he *was* really mad, he'd just shout, 'Fresh tea.'"

Vincent pulled her closer. Ashleigh smiled and wiped her face.

Nathan nodded, his eyes a mixture of sadness and bittersweet mirth. "Yeah, it stuck with me."

Awwwww. Reena's heart melted. What an awesome story and a way for Nathan and Ashleigh to stay connected to Scott. She sniffled and wrangled with her flourishing emotions for the man. There Nathan went again. Showing a piece of himself he usually kept hidden.

Remembering he had the observation skills of a spy, she uttered, "Bet that makes you popular on a construction site," to distract him from discovering too much. "I can just imagine you cutting a wrong wire and yelling 'Fresh tea' around the other macho men."

Nathan snorted. "Benefits of owning the company. I don't have to care what they say."

"Being the boss does have its advantages." Rummaging in her coat pocket, she triumphantly fished out a crumpled napkin from her favorite taco place. Turning, she cleared her nose. It didn't really matter if she swiped at the tears, the rain kept her face wet regardless. "I opened my art gallery downtown when I returned from college." Owning a business had its perks for sure, but sometimes always being responsible for everything weighed her down.

His dark brown eyes lit up and Nathan leaned a bit closer, intrigue and questions brewing in his expression.

Ashleigh cleared her throat again. "Um, Reena?" Her voice quavered. "Are we trapped on the mountain?"

That question sobered everyone instantly.

Reality crashed their time-out, pushing restart on their situation.

Jamming the used tissue into her pocket, Reena glanced at the forlorn supports holding against the rapids. Her eyes flicked to her backpack, then her stomach plunged. Her maps were gone. Sandy had asked to study them when they had taken the break. It hadn't occurred to Reena to grab them back when she realized the teens were missing. By now, the maps were in the van with the rest of the group, safe and dry. Everything they weren't.

Her mind raced, recalling what she could when she had planned the worship weekend. "The short answer is no."

"But…" Nathan prompted.

"But…there's not another bridge anywhere close." Her stomach twisted. Details from web sites and paper maps continued to pop into her mind, each adding a swivel until her stomach resembled an intricate knot.

"So, what does that mean?" Nathan asked, the light in his eyes dimming.

"That means we have to hike." Reena motioned toward the forest on their side.

Ashleigh peered at the trees. "For how long?"

"Well." Reena scratched her nose to stall, dreading the reception of her answer. "That depends on the route we take."

"You're being cagey," Nathan accused, lifting his chin.

He was absolutely right.

"Spill," Ashleigh demanded.

"Are we talking hours? Days? Weeks?" Nathan probed, not letting her get away with anything.

"I don't know." The headache that had subsided during their time-out roared back with a vengeance. Between the pounding in her skull and her acrobatic stomach, she had trouble remembering every element on the trails.

Blood seeping from some of the scrapes on her palms snagged her attention. She grimaced at the stinging and burning. Casually hiding her hands behind her back to keep the others from noticing, she continued. "With these conditions…" she trailed off.

"Guess."

Ashleigh's and Vincent's heads swiveled back and forth; this time, they landed on her, waiting for a response.

Clearing her throat, she ventured, "Maybe a day…but probably more like a day and a half."

Silence reigned, except for the storm.

Reena steeled her spine and met Nathan's penetrating stare with confidence…or at least a confident bluff. She hated any kind of confrontation with a passion.

"A day, but more like a day and a half," Nathan repeated.

"Yes." She waited for the explosion. Hopefully, Ashleigh and Vincent wouldn't be too scarred by this whole mess.

Nathan rubbed the bridge of his nose. "I don't even know what to say."

Shock slapped her mouth closed. She had thought for sure he'd let her have it. True, it wasn't her fault the storm veered north, nor had she caused the bridge to collapse, but Nathan had already told her he blamed her for Ashleigh and Vincent's disappearance. He had made it plain he thought her decision to exclude the chaperones from the scavenger hunt was dangerous and stupid. And now he was passing up the opportunity to make that dig again?

Her eyes narrowed on the confusing man. What was his game?

"What are we facing?" Nathan asked.

His tone was calm and logical, completely throwing her off-kilter. This time she wasn't so jazzed about uncovering another Nathan layer. She wasn't even sure if this was a layer or a trick to lure her in to relaxing before he pounced. *Now you're just being unfair.* She should take the gift and stop questioning it.

Right. *Positive thinking always soothes.* "*A lot* of walking. Miles and miles."

All three grimaced as if choreographed.

"That's it?" Nathan pushed.

"Um," she hedged. "The routes vary. At some point, we will face either a vertical climb or tackling rocks."

Chapter Eleven

Blood drained from Nathan's head and he blinked black spots. No way he heard right. The stress had to be messing with his ability to process words. Not only was the group forced to hike for *days* to escape the mountain, but they had to tackle a vertical climb or something with rocks?

"What?" Vincent asked, echoing Nathan's thought.

"Can you say that again?" Nathan focused intently on the disheveled redhead who confounded him and occupied way too many of his thoughts lately.

Reena shifted her hips. The cuts and dirt on her face reinforced the pain echoing in her hazel eyes. Guilt wriggled in the bottom of his heart. He only had to deal with a bruise over his kidney from a rock while she silently handled a litany of injuries.

"Which part do you want repeated?" Reena asked, her hands still oddly behind her back.

"Uh, all of it?" Nathan couldn't believe the latest twist to their circumstances. "At the very least, that last line you threw out."

"We will have a directional choice to make at some

point," Reena explained. "One path leads us to a ranger station, the other leads to the highway and hopefully a cell phone signal."

"You said something about a vertical climb or rocks," Nathan pressed, sensing she was being evasive again.

"I did."

Nathan was trying to be mature about the turn of events. Trying to keep a leash on the anger that sat right below the surface since Scott's death, but the fact remained they were in this position because of her decisions. He kept his opinion to himself this time, not wanting the teens to wig out any more than they were. Not easy to do. He hadn't had a thing to do with how they reached this point. She had planned and executed everything herself, regardless of his initial objections.

But none of that could matter now. He exhaled, forcing the blame game and antagonism to expel with the air. Just like working with different wire gauges on a project, he sparked a new connection in his mind. He'd work *with* Reena as much as possible. She had way more experience in the woods.

Little squiggles of doubt lingered…could he trust her decisions? Maybe she'd listen to his concerns this time around. If she explained what they faced, he could offer advice and they'd avoid another situation like this—

Thunder rolled its menace, echoing, but not as sharp as before.

"Everyone away from the water," Reena stated, maneuvering around him. "I'm not giving lightning a second chance to hit me."

His boots slid and sucked into the mud in his bid to catch up. Chagrin chapped his ego and an inferno lit his cheeks. *Duh, Nathan*. He made his living off electrical current. Water excelled at conducting electricity, yet this plucky woman had to school him on the basic principle. He peered over his shoulder to make sure his niece and Vincent were following, and to stall for time. He had to finish swallowing the ashy taste of embarrassment.

A trail he hadn't noticed the first time around opened three feet from where the bridge once stood. Vines encroached the space, but the vegetation allowed enough room for two people to walk abreast...very closely together. The path meandered through the forest, steadily inclining degree by degree. Deep rivulets carved into the mud overflowed with water, threatening to flood the path.

Uncaring, he invaded Reena's personal space, inhaling a small waft of strawberries. He dared not imagine what he smelled like. Fingers crossed, she'd scent only wet cloth and nature. He stayed beside her, step for step. Well, step for limp. "Slow down." His conscience pricked. She hadn't really taken a break since the tree incident.

She ignored him. Shocker.

Jagged gray rocks—some his height, some bigger— began replacing the vegetation crowding the edges of the trail. Lichen or moss, he really didn't understand the difference, covered the surface, adding a creepy slimy effect. Evergreens—he had no clue the species—fifty feet and taller grew behind and on top of the rocks, driving home the "stranded in the woods" effect. Maybe in sunlight, he'd feel better but, right now, it all just reinforced why he never explored forests.

"Reena." He clasped her biceps, praying he wasn't pressing on one of her injuries. "Stop."

"Why?" she demanded, halting due to his unrelenting grip. "We don't have to make a decision on which route to take for a while now, so there's no sense arguing. We need to keep going."

The pastiness of her skin decided it. "You need to rest." He turned to the teens. "Vincent, can you hand me the water bottle from Reena's pack?"

"Oh, thank you!" Ashleigh cried dramatically. "I'm so thirsty and starved, too."

Excellent parenting, Nathan. He should have realized the kids needed refueling. Fear and running for cover drained the body. Turning his back on his niece, he thumbed toward his backpack. "Ashleigh, energy bars are in the small front section."

She tore into his bag while Vincent offered the water to Reena. The youth director eyed it as if it would bite her, then sighed heavily.

"Thanks." Reena took it and unscrewed the cap. After gulping a quarter down, she thrust it toward Vincent. "Drink. You need it, too. And you'll find bars in my pack if you're also hungry."

Smacking Nathan like a baseball to the head, he realized Ashleigh and Vincent had no provisions. They had left their backpacks with the chaperones before the scavenger hunt.

Nathan scrubbed his face out of habit. Gross. Smearing dirt into his pores could not be healthy. Obviously he had noticed neither teen had a pack but it hadn't dawned on him until this moment what that meant. "I'm so dense."

"I could've told you that," Reena quipped without missing a beat.

"Ha." Nathan waved toward the teens. "By now, their packs are dry and comfortable in the van with the rest of the group. They have no food, water, clothes, or even basic toiletries."

"Yeah, I know." Reena shook her head at Vincent's trying to pass the water back to her. The teen then thrust a freshly opened energy bar at her and stubbornly waited until she took it.

"I wish *I* had realized." Nathan hated that he wasn't as quick on the draw as Ms. Sunshine.

"Why?" Reena answered, chomping on a bar filled with almonds and chocolate chips. "Would it have changed anything?"

"No," he answered sullenly. But that was not the point. He was responsible for Ashleigh. Understanding what she needed to survive was something he should know. "This day just gets better and better," he muttered.

Reena stiffened but didn't respond. Instead, she began trudging on the path again.

"I'm so sorry, Uncle Nathan." Ashleigh handed him an unwrapped peanut butter protein bar. "This is all my fault."

Nathan exhaled. "Not *everything* is your fault, but yes, you own a large part of our predicament."

Her shoulders slumped and her gaze hit the ground.

He grabbed the bar. "You can stop apologizing."

Ashleigh snapped her face up, hope filling her features. "Am I forgiven?"

Munching on the bar, he drew out the moment just to be ornery. "Yes."

"I love you," she squealed and hugged him, almost knocking the protein bar into the mud.

"I love you, too, squirt, but," he cautioned, returning the hug with one arm, "punishment is still forthcoming."

"Fair." She bounced away, practically skipping to Vincent, who high-fived her.

Shaking his head at the confusing girl, he marched toward Reena. Since when did a teenager become chipper with a looming punishment? Shouldn't she be dreading the consequences? He'd never understand his niece.

Splashes and plops resumed behind him, letting him know the teens followed.

In three bites, he finished the bar and wished for another. A late lunch had been planned at the break after the scavenger hunt but, obviously, that hadn't happened.

The path had transformed from sections of broken rocks and vegetation to two long, gray, striated faces as if sections had broken away a long time ago. The sides were now twelve to fifteen feet high and, despite the rocky terrain above, evergreens still brimmed along with verdant shrubs growing where they could find space. Some of the foliage had bright flowers or weird blossom things. Loose leaves and other detritus smothered the lichen/moss-covered rock and rode thin little waterfalls onto the trail.

Reaching Reena's side, he exclaimed, "Would you just stop?" Exasperation at constantly chasing after the mind-boggling woman showing.

She side-eyed him again. Not slowing one bit. Of course.

"We have a long way to go and only so much daylight," she pragmatically answered from her hunch within the obnoxiously bright raincoat.

It took everything he had not to grab her again. He had never been so tactual with anyone before, outside of his family. He wished he knew what brought out the tendency. He'd strangle it into submission. Jogging—

more like slogging and slipping—he managed to pull ahead. Pivoting, he planted his feet into the mud directly in her path.

"Nathan," she growled, halting at the last moment. For a second, he thought she might literally walk all over him. "Move. While daylight might be more of a reference than actual light in this storm, we still need to take advantage of it."

"Hands." He pointed at the appendages hidden in her pockets. "Let's see them."

"We don't have time for this." She made to go around him, but he blocked her effort.

"No." He refused to back down. "We don't have time for them to become infected. Hold them out."

Vincent already had Reena's backpack resting on his boots. He rummaged in the large compartment, then whipped out a plastic case with a red cross on top.

"I can do it." Reena went for the first-aid kit, but Nathan snatched it first.

"Ms. Sunshine," he stated softly, bending until they were eye level. Never in his life had he been on such an emotional roller coaster. This tiny package of energy had him laughing one minute then ready to yell the next. "Would you *please* let me help you?"

"We haven't even traveled a mile!" Red flared across her cheeks and she puffed out air. "There are more important things—"

"Your health is just as important as anyone else's in this group. So stop with the excuses and the martyr bit." Nathan waved at Vincent. "Come here." Once the teen stood beside Reena, he instructed, "Arch your back."

Vincent's eyebrows drew down but he did as asked.

"Flatten your palms beneath Vincent. He makes an excellent umbrella."

The teen chuckled and puffed wider to utilize his entire frame and raincoat.

"Grrrrrr," she growled, rolling her eyes.

Nathan flattened his stare—not easy to do with that adorable sound rumbling his way.

Reena *finally* followed the direction.

The cuts and scrapes looked red and puffy. "Yikes." He carefully opened the case.

Ashleigh maneuvered to stand beside him, took the box, then arched forward. Holding it open beneath her, she grinned. "I'm your umbrella, Nurse Porter."

Smirking, he plucked up the hydrogen peroxide bottle. "Ready for the fun to begin?" He didn't wait. He cleaned the injuries. Her palms trembled and she sucked in a breath, but didn't say a word. He added ointment to the sores, then wrapped gauze from knuckles to wrists. Spying a pair of small latex gloves, he began inserting one over her hand.

"We should save those—"

"The rain will soak your bandages in a heartbeat." He continued working the tight rubber over her fingers, while Vincent helped with the other glove. "Who knows what will filter through."

Inspecting her newly treated and covered wounds, Reena grumbled, "Can we go now? I'd like to log quite a few miles today and, at the rate we're going, we'll be lucky to surpass two."

The thunder continued to unload, adding its part to nature's soundtrack.

"What's the password?" Nathan prompted, his lips lifting in a smile on their own.

"Seriously?" Reena shifted from foot to foot. "How about, 'if you don't move out of my way this second, I'll run you over.'"

"Too long." Nathan lifted his face to the rain and let it wet his mouth. Why was he teasing her? More important, why did it feel like flirting? He couldn't handle adding another person in his life right now and, besides, this woman was all wrong for him. She was too…happy, too…into finding the silver lining and stuff. Too trusting in God. He wanted someone grounded in the real world. Someone serious, who—

Something scratched across his outer chest. He snapped his chin down to find Reena hobbling around him. "That's cheating."

"I never agreed to play fair," she shot back over her shoulder.

Ashleigh and Vincent grinned at him. Pivoting to avoid their perceptive faces, he started after Reena. Again.

Chapter Twelve

Eyeing the thin streams of water and sediment flowing over the uneven rock, Reena's calves burned with the constant incline. Just what she needed to add to her misery.

What's the password? Nathan's question replayed over and over. The twinkle in his eyes when he threw out that curveball had knocked her off-center. Not only did Mr. Porter have a surprising sense of humor, he had a playful side. Fascinating. And another mystery layer revealed. *What's the password?* Those teasing words accompanied an image of rain pouring over the man, yet his boyish grin emanated as if it were a sunny day. The sudden urge to flirt and tease him back had surged and she'd fought the impulse by doing the opposite. By pretending to be huffy that he'd blocked her way. *Real mature, Reena.*

Towering spruces flourishing among the rocky terrain bounced their branches in the wind and cast a gloom that the storm's black clouds didn't help.

What in the world was going on with her heart? Nathan Porter was *not* her ideal soul mate candidate. She saw herself with someone who embraced God and the church. Someone who focused on the positives—

Wait. Back up. Soul mate candidate? Where had that thought come from? And when had Nathan even become a consideration? Yes, he had intrigued her from the moment he'd stepped into the church and, yes, she constantly watched him from afar—in a total non-stalker way. And yes, the man enticed her curiosity to uncover the person behind the palpable wall, but she was more like a sleuth solving a mystery, not evaluating an eternal partner.

The knot in her stomach twisted. Why oh why had she let her mouth toss that stupid coy comment over her shoulder to his cheating accusation? Her mind should have vetoed it. It potentially encouraged more teasing… or, dare she admit, flirting.

Her head pounded in time with her steps. Partially buried rocks protruded haphazardly in the mud, waiting to trip an unsuspecting traveler. Water swept around them, causing ripples that helped her spot the pending menaces. "Watch out for the rocks in the trail," she called as loudly as her migraine allowed.

Shoving her hands in her pockets, she grimaced at the snug latex gloves. They trapped the heat, but she wouldn't take them off. As much as she hated losing precious daylight, Nathan had been right to treat the injuries. A shiver stole through her veins. Whenever he focused his full attention on her, her systems went haywire. The urge to squirm under his gaze warred with the desire to blush and smile like a sappy maiden, which warred with the combative yearning to face him head-on.

Heavy boots splashing in water steadily hijacking the path gave away Nathan's position. Though she doubted he was trying to be stealthy in the narrow chute. Their elbows practically touched when he drew abreast, his insistence to stay *right* beside her still strong.

A part of her wanted to speed up to keep some distance between them. This crazy notion about him being a possible soul mate freaked her out. She'd never had that thought about anyone before and she didn't know how to handle it.

Her epiphany, or whatever the unwelcome insight was called, had another drawback besides its existence. She was now *aware* of Nathan. Her senses tuned into him like a satellite deciphering signals. The way he tackled the path and how he held his body. The expression on his face and the ability to guess his mood. Just him in general. *Agh*. She felt like a teenager discovering an awkward crush. It had to stop. Now.

Thou dost protest too much. Great. Now she had William Shakespeare horning in on her thoughts.

Fighting the inclination to increase her pace, much to her hips' rejoicing, she remained next to Nathan, gritting her teeth against the assailing speculations and perceptions.

Find the silver lining… Oh! She was just loopy from hitting her head. That was all. Her mind clung to the reason for her sudden insanity. Her heart thumped in protest, but she and her brain ignored the organ.

Wind whipped through the trees, funneling into the chute. Loose, dead sections of branches above plummeted to the earth like missiles. Splashes and bangs echoed as the debris landed, luckily on no one's head. As if to annoy her, the gust carried the scent of wet cloth along with something musky and male. Nathan. She had been catching traces of his soap or aftershave all day. Wishing she could find it unpleasant, she snorted to clear her nostrils of the rich, attractive smell.

Lightning lit up the dark clouds, filtering light through the gaps in the canopy.

Reena winced in reflex and started counting the seconds... *Four, five, six—*

Thunder cracked, then grumbled.

Exhaling, her shoulders dropped from crowding her ears. The lightning was a little over a mile away.

"I think the storm's moving out." Nathan dodged a rock, momentarily pressing his muscled arm against her.

"You're right about the storm," she answered, eyeing the increasing water overtaking the trail to keep from noticing anything about the contact.

"I am?"

"Yep," she agreed, going for casual. Her awareness needed to calm down and scram. "I used to be afraid of storms," she explained, hunching against the gusts driving the rain into her. "Until my dad taught me a game when I was six. He made a show of calculating the distance by timing the seconds between the lightning and the thunder."

"I've heard of that." Nathan's right arm dunked through the little waterfalls streaming over the sides. "Isn't it something like every second is a mile?"

"Close." The trail curved to the right. "I'm not an expert by any means—"

"I know the answer," Vincent interjected, his voice bouncing off the rocks. "I did a whole science fair project on weather one year."

Reena motioned for the teen to answer. She could've spouted the internet article, but she loved it when one of her youths took pride in his education.

Vincent hustled closer. "It takes five seconds for sound to travel a mile," he explained, his tone warming to the topic. "That's much slower than light."

"Of course, temperature and humidity could throw off the speed of traveling sound," Ashleigh chimed in, grinning, "but five seconds is great for estimation."

Nathan snapped his head to peer over his shoulder.

Ashleigh beamed at him. "I got an A in Earth Science." Her shoulders waggled. "I loved that class."

"Let's keep that sentiment for all your classes this coming year," Nathan encouraged, "and we'll talk about you getting your learner's permit."

Reena winced at the loud shriek and clapping dance. The incline leveled noticeably—

Grabbing Nathan's forearm, she yanked hard.

"Wha—" He whipped forward and his off-balance leg slammed down, hitting the tip of a rock that would've had him sprawling. "Oh. Thanks."

Her palms wailed and her body protested the jostling, but she ignored them. Her attention riveted on Nathan's ears reddening and his adjusting his T-shirt nonchalantly, like nothing happened. The male ego was fascinating. Infuriating at times, but fascinating.

Vincent's snicker died at Nathan's glare and he continued. "Where was I? Oh. Once you have the number of seconds between the lightning and the thunder, you divide by five. The answer is the number of miles away the lightning is."

"In this case—" Reena took over "—a little over a mile. The seconds between the two have been growing progressively longer. And I'm grateful for that." She shuddered. "I'm done with electricity attempting to sabotage me."

"If only this rain let up," Ashleigh grouched, splattering liquid in time with her stomps.

Reena wholeheartedly agreed. She forgot what it felt like to be dry. And clean. And pain-free. She missed not having grime coating places it had no business touching, or walking normally, or not aching...everywhere.

The curve ended...

"You have got to be kidding me." Nathan slowed.

Reena blinked, her pace matching Nathan's until she eventually halted.

"Did the storm do that?" Vincent asked, his big body hovering behind hers.

"I...think...so." Reena could barely process the sight twenty feet ahead.

A fifty-foot spruce had toppled over, blocking the trail. The top rested on more spruces and pines filling the other side, its angle perfect enough for countless branches covered in evergreen needles to fill the space between the high-walled rock trail. As if ripped out of the ground, Reena could spy a piece of exposed section of the enormous root system with chunks of dirt and soil still clinging despite the rain trying to wash it away. With the once healthy tree on its side, a crater now existed in place of the roots. But a crater couldn't contain the continuous drenching. Sure enough, water overflowed in a torrent, rushing toward open ground...the trail below it. Their trail. Water flooded the area and escaped down the path they had just climbed. It explained why a creek existed where a trail should've been.

"How do we cross that?" Ashleigh asked the million-dollar question, clutching the base of her throat. Her gaze flitted between the barricade, Nathan, and Reena.

Nathan searched their immediate surroundings and Reena knew his conclusion. It had to be the same as hers. *Not easily.*

Chapter Thirteen

❧

Nathan flung his hand toward the latest disaster. "Is Mother Nature conspiring against us?"

"Apparently." Reena chewed on her bottom lip and stared at the downed tree.

"Do we have to go back?" Vincent asked, shifting sideways.

"It wouldn't do much good," Reena answered, stepping closer to the obstacle. "This is the only trail for miles until it splits later."

Ashleigh put her hands on her hips. "We could make our own path like we did before."

"In this storm? I wouldn't risk doing that again." Reena shook her head, wisps of her hair fluttering out of the hood, leaves still woven within. "The terrain is dangerous and unpredictable on a perfect day. It'd be foolish to attempt it a second time."

Nathan held his cell phone up, swinging it left and right. "Nothing." He dropped his arm. He hadn't expected a signal, but the disappointment still existed.

Water pooled close to the top of his ankle-high boots

and swirled as it hustled past. "Is it me or is it getting deeper?"

Reena whirled and Vincent grunted. The teen jogged back down the trail, staying mostly in the middle, then rounded the curve out of view. The steady sloshing of his steps was just as good as having a visual since the cadence meant he was all right.

Ashleigh marched toward Reena, her face a mix of determination and fear.

Pride swelled for his niece. Meeting the calamity head-on showed an encouraging level of maturity. Maybe her screw-up earlier had taught her something after all.

Splashing grew louder and Vincent popped back in sight. "You want the bad news or the…well, that's it. Bad news."

As if it would be anything else. "I'd *love* to hear bad news," Nathan cracked dryly. "It's been ages since we had any."

Vincent grinned at the joke, but his face didn't hold any mirth. The teen kept going until he reached Reena.

Guess he should join the party. After all, there was bad news to be had. Who'd want to miss that?

With the foursome gathered close, Nathan swiped his hands through his hair. He didn't shudder at the grit coating his fingers any longer.

"Don't keep us in suspense!" Ashleigh demanded, whapping Vincent on the arm.

Vincent eyed her, then met Reena's troubled gaze. "In the middle of the curve—" he jabbed a thumb over his shoulder. "Mud, limbs, and small rocks are sliding off—" he motioned to the top of the fifteen-foot-tall rock "—on the left side."

"What?" Ashleigh jolted.

"How deep?" Reena asked, the furrow between her eyes increasing.

"Deep enough to act like a dam." Vincent helpfully expanded his arms to imitate his words in case someone didn't know the definition. "It's spread across the trail and building up."

Thunder boomed and the wind howled in response.

The toppled tree shook, then *creaked*, raising the hair on Nathan's arms.

"Move!" Reena shouted, waving frantically.

The tree precariously perched across the trail rocked and bobbed, falling…in their direction.

Nathan curled an arm around Ashleigh's waist and lifted at the same moment he pivoted, running as fast as he could in the muddy water. Heart leaping into its favorite position in his throat, he prayed he wouldn't choke on the organ or find a hidden rock the hard way. Or both.

The sound of a wet explosion, like an old-school cannonball into a pool, echoed. Nathan jerked, whipping Ashleigh to the side. She yelped and clung to his forearm, her nails digging in. Loud groaning followed the splash and a wave of water hit his calves. Out of the corner of his eye, he spied Reena scuttling as fast as her lopsided gait allowed. Vincent hovered close, his arms at the ready to catch her.

The sudden silence rang louder than the noise.

Nathan froze, grunting when Ashleigh's heels connected with his shins.

"Put me down." She squirmed and Nathan instantly let go. More water drenched his legs from his niece's landing.

As if they were magnets, his eyes were drawn to the downed evergreen. The top of it had wrenched free of the trees once supporting it and had rolled forward. Instead of the trunk lying at an angle, it now fell flush on top of the rock. Before, the group might have had success wiggling through the branches, but not anymore. Not only was the tree about fifty feet in length, it had a forty-foot total width—twenty feet ranging out from the trunk all around. Those branches now sloped down, the ends crushing against the earth. Some branches still pointed skyward, but a lot were drooping together. Pine cones, needles, and limbs twisted into a tangled mass, blocking everything. Even light couldn't shine through.

Reena panted, holding her hips and wincing visibly. She halted next to him and his hands itched to take the brunt of her weight to ease the pain, but he balled them into fists instead. What was with him? He had already touched her beyond his usual threshold. If he didn't find a way to quell the constant inexplicable urge, he'd find more excuses to connect. And he didn't want to keep gravitating toward her.

"Uh, guys?" Ashleigh kicked her feet. "I think the water's getting higher."

Nathan's gaze shot to his own boots and found his niece was right. He could no longer see his socks. "Fantastic," he muttered, swiping the scruff on his jaw. "Maybe if we stick around long enough, we can swim over the tree." How much more absurd could this fiasco get?

"If only," Reena responded, tossing her hood back. She lifted her face to the rain and closed her eyes.

No way had he just heard defeat from Ms. Sunshine. "Are—"

"Okay," Reena said with the enthusiasm of a cheerleader on game day, cutting off his question about her health. "We need to assess our options."

Yikes. He'd never played sports in school, but he'd seen enough cheerleader-to-crowd interactions to know fake rallying when he heard it. Were they in more trouble than he realized? The hair on his arms that only had just calmed down slowly rose straight.

"We can't go back the way we came," Vincent offered. "Unless you want to put making our own trail back on the table." The hope brimming in his eyes was hard to miss.

"Nope." Reena popped the *P* like a tab on an aluminum can. "Still too dangerous." She fixed the yellow hood back over her hair and studied the rock and tree. "We'll have to climb."

"You've done that before, right?" Nathan eyed the same terrain, wishing it hadn't come to this. So far, this worship weekend hadn't been anything he'd signed up for. Climbing trees had *not* been on the agenda. It was just going to highlight how out of his depth he truly was. Give him a high-tech engineering challenge and he'd dominate...but trees...

"Can't say I've been in this exact situation," Reena admitted, moving closer to a mass of limbs, "but I have scaled rocks and climbed trees in my life."

An image of a younger Reena jumped into his mind. She had scrapes on her freckled legs and arms, but those didn't stop her from latching on to a thick branch and pulling herself up like a monkey. Smiling at the sun beaming off her auburn hair in the scene, he could only shake his head. He'd bet she had always been adventurous.

"Do you think it's stable?"

Vincent's question dissolved the absurd musing and

grounded Nathan into reality. It did him no good collecting pieces of Reena. He had another person to think about now. Ashleigh weighed in heavily on any relationship—

Stop. Why was he thinking about a relationship in context to Reena? *Focus, Nathan.*

"We're about to find out," Reena answered, grabbing on to a three-inch limb with both gloved hands.

Chapter Fourteen

"**D**on't!"

Reena had already started pushing when Nathan shouted. Stiff needles pressed against the layers on her palms, poking her injuries like spikes. Part of the tree's limb bent with the force, its flexibility an excellent defense against nature but not a great source for holding weight.

An unyielding bar hooked around her abdomen and yanked her backward. Her feet flew up and her back slammed against a hard surface. The twigs and needles whipped through her palms and the air froze in her lungs. Jostling up and down, her brain sloshed in her skull, and she couldn't process a thought beyond watching the spruce bounce in her vision.

Just as fast, everything stopped. It took another second for her mind to catch up, then she slapped her hands against the bar...a soft yet hard bar with hair, connected to a man she was uncomfortably aware of. "Nathan!" She clawed at his hold. "What are you doing? Let me go."

"What am *I* doing?" he retorted, setting her down in water now at her lower calves, five feet from the tree. "Are you crazy? You don't pull on an unstable tree!"

She gained her balance and whirled on the obtuse man. "I *didn't* pull on it. I'm not stupid."

His eyes snapped. "I've got to wonder if you knocked your head harder than I thought."

"Hey!" She jabbed at him, her finger bouncing off his chest. "Leave my head out of this."

Nathan blinked and Reena cringed at her asinine comeback.

"You know what I mean," she retorted, glaring at the rain plinking into the filling area like a bathtub. "I know better than to pull on a fifty-plus-foot tree that just rolled over."

"If you weren't pulling, then how were you testing the stability?" Nathan's fingers tightened on his waist, the skin whitening.

Reena lifted her hands and blinked at the ragged condition. Pieces of latex dangled limply from the holes torn into the gloves and green needles dug into the ripped gauze with dirt lines running throughout. "Great! Look what you did." She flipped her palms face-out near her head.

"I…" He slammed his mouth closed, then tried again. "I thought you were going to get crushed." He swiped at his drenched hairline as he flitted his gaze from hers to something behind her.

"So you swooped in to save me," Reena finished, not sure if she was insulted at his lack of faith in her or flattered he put himself in presumed danger to protect her. Maybe a little of both. Deciding to focus on the positive of the two, she relented. "Thank you for 'rescuing' me." Her fingers formed air quotes of their own volition.

He blew out a breath then motioned to her hands. "Sorry about that."

Reena shrugged. "It was bound to happen anyway. They were too fragile for the forest."

"Awww." Ashleigh placed her hands beneath her chin and fluttered her eyelashes. "You two kiss and make up now."

Heat seared Reena's face at the same time Nathan pointed at his niece. "Shut it."

Ashleigh cackled, slapping her chest. "They're so cute." She leaned against Vincent's biceps. "Look at them, all embarrassed."

"You are just asking for trouble, Ash," Vincent sang, though he had a Cheshire cat smile.

"You got that right," Nathan shot back, crossing his arms. The rain didn't diminish the imposing stance one bit. "Talk about embarrassment, I'm sure I can think of *something* a certain mouthy squirt wouldn't want publicized." His gaze bore into Ashleigh, then flicked to Vincent and back.

Ashleigh straightened so fast she almost fell against the rock. "Uncle. Nathan!"

He smirked, his grin growing wider and evil. "What?" he asked innocently.

Reena giggled until she couldn't stop the laugh. Vincent's eyebrows shot high and he swiveled his gaze between the two Porters, obviously hoping for a clue. That only made Reena laugh harder. The two teens had undeniable crushes on each other yet neither had figured it out. Nathan's extreme observational skills had struck again, reminding Reena that he saw a lot more than a typical person.

"Okay, okay." Ashleigh held up both hands in surrender. "You win. I'm sorry for teasing. No kissing. No making up. Got it."

"And no kissing for you until you're twenty-one," Nathan commanded, glowering at both teens.

Ashleigh's jaw dropped and Vincent slammed his gaze to the water, his mouth opening, then closing with no sound.

"Harsh," Reena whispered, feeling sorry for Vincent. He had to be mortified. He was so serious that most people didn't realize it covered shyness.

"Not even a little," Nathan murmured, relaxing his pose. "She won't date, either, if I have my say in it."

Rumbling thunder overhead punctuated his proclamation.

"Vincent's a great guy." Reena turned to face the tree. "Give him a chance." She peered over the shoulder opposite the teens and kept her voice low. "He did save Ashleigh from drowning, don't forget."

Nathan shuddered. "I'll *never* be able to forget."

Satisfied she'd done what she could to help Vincent win Nathan's favor, she faced the real obstacle. The evergreen blockade. That moment of laughter had been a nice respite from her fatigue. *Ugh.* She had tried to rally earlier but all it did was hide her weariness behind false cheer…and upset Nathan, if she'd read his tight lips and stiff posture right. Staring at the behemoth ahead, she inwardly sighed. The task wasn't insurmountable but her injuries made it feel that way. On any other day, she'd be bouncing to tackle the beast.

Her skin grew warm and she shifted under Nathan's piercing gaze. "Are you going to physically be able to climb out of here?"

Wow. He did not pull punches. She eyed the water rising, then the tree, everywhere but his eyes. "Yes. I don't have a choice." The doubts spooling inside grew and she knew Mr. Eagle Eyes would notice in a heartbeat. Rubbing her forehead, she glared at the tattered latex. Why hadn't she packed her rugged leather gloves? Just because she hadn't planned any events where she'd need them didn't mean she shouldn't have been prepared. They would've been great to protect her palms, but she had wanted the space for bug spray and sunblock instead.

Reena moved closer to the mass. "Spruces are not ideal for climbing."

Nathan grabbed a thin branch near his knee and waggled it. "Will it hold us?"

"It should." Reena prayed she was right. "The three-inch branches are really flexible, but see how sections of them are crossed together or stacked? That should help lend strength."

"I have an idea," Vincent interjected. "We split up. That way all four of us won't strain one section to the point of breaking."

"Like, two climb against the left side while two climb the right?" Ashleigh clarified.

"Exactly." Vincent nodded, tightening the backpack.

"I don't like it," Nathan announced, scowling at the spruce. "Sticking together allows us to help each other if someone needs it."

"How about this?" Reena tried for a compromise. "Since I'm the one with the most experience, I'll go first. If it's strong, then we can go from there, but if it's weak, we'll split up."

"But you're the most injured," Nathan stuttered. "How are you going to grip a branch or pull yourself up?"

"Same as if I was in fourth place," she shot back. "No matter what, I have to climb. There's no getting around it."

To end the debate, Reena carefully plucked a path through the mass. The last thing she wanted was Nathan going "heroic" again. Doing something caveman like tossing her over his shoulder before tackling the tree. She could just picture him getting it into his head that he had to help *her* instead of Ashleigh.

Spreading her arms for balance, she hobbled and wiggled across until she reached a mass that had both stacked branches and two crossing at one point. It exaggerated the pain in her hip, but she was determined to hold her own.

Chapter Fifteen

"Uncle Nathan," Ashleigh hissed, pulling on his arm. "You can't let her climb the tree *alone*." She flung a hand up. "Go help her."

Nathan freed his abused appendage. "Did you hear her ask for help?" His conscience pricked at his response. He hated to see Reena in such pain, but his first priority was Ashleigh. And didn't that just spark a whole new war inside him? He had no business even *thinking* about aiding Reena before Ashleigh, yet battle lines began forming anyway.

"Ugggggh!" Ashleigh cried dramatically. "Guys are soooo dense!"

"That's a valuable life lesson you should remember, Ashleigh," Reena called over her shoulder, proving she could hear every word.

Great. Before Nathan could protest or defend his intelligence, Ashleigh stormed forward.

"Ashleigh Lynn Porter," Nathan barked, missing the back of her/his raincoat by millimeters. "Stop right there."

She raised a hand in a wave, but kept going.

What was with the females in his life lately? He was a macho fool when he did try to help and dense when he didn't. "Have I transported into an alternate dimension?"

"You took me with you if you did," Vincent replied, swiping his face, then shaking the wetness away only for the rain to soak his skin again.

Nathan snorted. "Do you know how to get us back?" Sighing, he marched after his niece. "Come on. We might as well stay together."

Ashleigh stepped from one branch clump to another with the ease of a tightrope walker. He envied her confident stride. His looked more like a moose trying to stay upright on ice. And he'd already learned a lesson about seemingly innocent nature. His aching side could attest to that.

They reached Reena, who had managed to progress two feet up the limbs. Not exactly swift, but that could work in his favor. If he didn't have to rush, he could keep an eye on Ashleigh without breaking his neck.

Ashleigh on his right and Vincent on his left imitated Reena's crouched pose. Nathan did his best to follow suit, his arms flapping to keep from falling on his butt. The three of them grabbed on to branches in front of them with Nathan closest to Reena.

"Way to stick to the plan, guys." Reena shook her head.

Ashleigh confidently readjusted her grip. "I'm going to rule this. I'm super boss at the rope bridge challenge at the Renaissance Faire and carnivals."

"You didn't beat me last year," Vincent corrected. "Until you win, *I* maintain the bragging rights, Ash."

"Not for long, Clarky," she retorted, adding a *y* to the end of Vincent's last name.

"Whoever makes it to the top without falling first, wins." Vincent threw down the gauntlet.

"I don't think so," Nathan barked.

"Actually—" Reena grinned at his niece "—Ashleigh does rule on the rope bridge. I've seen it firsthand."

"And I've seen a video," Nathan retorted, bristling for no sensible reason. "A thick rope ladder anchored at the top and bottom are no comparison to tree limbs bending and moving."

Reena shifted her hips and Nathan caught the grimace.

"I disagree," Ashleigh countered. "The rope is tied to a small iron circle and steeply angled. It moves so much that that's the point. You have to master balancing while climbing to the next rung."

"Vincent," Reena said just as Nathan opened his mouth.

"Straight-up truth time," she demanded. "No lies or swagger. Do you truly believe you can climb up this, like the bridge, *safely*?"

What the…? Nathan's lips thinned. Reena could call for a vote but he was not done weighing in.

The serious expression filling Vincent's face impressed Nathan. The teen didn't scoff or puff up with self-importance. Instead, he gazed up the length of the tree, then back to Reena. "Yes. I think it's comparable. But I want to be next to Ash."

Oh, the boy was playing hardball, saying the right thing.

Reena swished her hand. "Pick your branches."

"No one move," Nathan ordered, taking a second to eye both teens.

Vincent froze mid-hunch.

"Uncle Nathan," Ashleigh whined. "I can *do* this."

"Just like you could go on the scavenger hunt with no issues?" he shot back, the line out before he realized he harbored it.

Ashleigh's jaw slammed closed and her face flared red. "I said I was sorry." She swallowed hard. "And this is different. I've done something like this before."

Nathan sighed. "You're right. You have apologized and I accepted." He tightened his grip on the branches, the bark digging in deep. "But this time you won't have any cushiony mats or straw beneath you. You fall, you break something."

"Whether you're beside her or not—" Reena waded in "—that principle remains."

And didn't that statement shut down his argument? Nathan inhaled against the fight still brewing inside. His job was to protect Ashleigh, but the forest kept testing his ability to perform the role.

"Keep going, Vincent," Reena encouraged.

The teen scratched his chin and warily eyed Nathan. "If you really object, we won't do it, but I'm sure we can reach the top without hurting anything. Ash and I will help each other if we get stuck. Okay?"

The earnestness on his face made Nathan concede. The kid knew how to present an argument. He logged that fact into a mental file to watch out for in the future.

"Fine," Nathan grumbled. "But don't get crazy with this race. It's better to tie and reach the top in one piece than break a leg and lose. Got it?"

"Woot!" Ashleigh shouted and Vincent continued moving.

While the teens were distracted, Nathan eased onto the same grouping as Reena. Turning sideways, he sat as best he could and used his legs as an anchor. The water and mud didn't faze him anymore. The tent strapped to the bottom of his backpack actually gave him a wider base to spread his weight. "You can stop hiding the pain," he whispered. "Lean on me. I can tell you're about to pass out."

Three beats of silence later, she muttered, "Why do you have to be so observant?"

"Survival skill growing up with an older brother who loved pranks." Nathan grinned, remembering one that involved clear plastic wrap and the toilet seat. Scott had almost gotten him with that in the dead of night. If it hadn't been for the moon casting a weird light through the bathroom window, Nathan would have made a mess.

"Definitely some stories there," Reena grumbled, maneuvering slowly.

Vincent hunkered into position on Ashleigh's other side.

"You two discuss strategies for a minute, okay?" Nathan instructed, to give Reena more time to settle into position. "Take this seriously."

Receiving their agreement, he braced for Reena's weight. She edged down beside him, her back divided between his arm and backpack. He bit the inside of his cheeks to stop a comment about her ragged sigh. As much as she frustrated him, confused him, and plagued his interest, she impressed him, too. She continued doing what had to be done without complaint or having a breakdown. Again, he wasn't sure he'd be so gracious. And his last girlfriend wouldn't have even offered to come on the trip, let alone search for teens in these conditions.

"You two ready?" Reena asked, leaning heavier against Nathan.

"It's not exactly going to be an even race." Vincent

thumbed over his shoulder. "I'm wearing a backpack, but Ash needs all the advantages she can get."

Nathan snickered at his niece's indignant scowl.

"It's *on*, Clarky."

"We're going to keep watch from here," Nathan responded. He wanted Reena to have as much time as possible to rest and if that coincidently put off his turn to climb, all the better.

His niece shot him a thumbs-up. "You going to record this?"

"No way." Nathan shuddered. "I'm pretty sure this could get me blackballed in most parenting circles. No proof, it's hearsay."

"That's why you're my favorite uncle."

"Ha. I'm your only uncle." The slice of pain that slashed his heart competed with the warmth at the declaration. The past six months had been all about learning to swim in the deep end before he drowned. Sounded like he was doing something right.

"On your mark," Reena trilled.

Their heads snapped forward, determination bristling.

"Get set." She waited a beat. "Go!"

Chapter Sixteen

Nathan's heart lurched into his throat *again*.

Ashleigh and Vincent began climbing. They hadn't taken off like kamikazes, but he didn't expect the complacent ascent to last long. He knew Ashleigh, and once she got her bearings, she'd turn up the speed.

With every movement, the branches shook and bowed deeper, but held. For now.

"Do you think Ashleigh and Vincent will ever figure out their mutual crush?" Reena asked with no hint of the white-knuckling he experienced.

"Uh, yeah, I do," he answered, dividing his focus. "It'll happen way too soon for my comfort."

"Come on." Reena pressed against him then eased. "Admit it. You like Vincent."

His gaze remained glued to the teens. Hand over hand, Vincent steadily climbed. He spread his feet at points to keep his balance, the backpack working against him at times. The torrential rain didn't seem to be a factor for the teen. Nathan knew in his gut the exact opposite would be his fate. It seemed like God really wanted him to learn a lesson…the hardest way possible. He shut that thought down before the anger could take hold. Way too many "lessons" lately had God's name all over them, and he couldn't handle any more.

To refocus his mind, he studied Vincent's technique, trying to memorize every movement and shift. He also had to schlep a pack and needed the pointers.

Huh. That was impressive. Ashleigh gripped a branch in her left hand while reaching for a new grouping on the right. She crab-walked over and continued climbing, keeping pace with Vincent. Neither seemed to falter and, outside of the hair-raising branch creaking and tree shaking, they were almost at the top.

Reena bumped his calf. "You that stubborn to admit it?"

Admit...? Oh. Yeah. Vincent. "I'm impressed, if I'm going to be honest. His and Ashleigh's different personalities complement each other's, but their realizing they like each other gives me an ulcer."

She glanced over her shoulder, her eyebrow lifting. "Why?"

"Once Ashleigh and Vincent stop dancing around their attraction, they might want to do something about it."

"Oh." Her cheeks flared a bright red and she ducked her head. "I get it."

He cleared his throat, scrabbling to change the uncomfortable topic. "I've noticed you're a little overprotective of Vincent. Why is that?"

She shrugged, running fingers over a set of needles. "I don't know. Ever since he started attending church and eventually my classes, he'd always been so quiet and serious. He never talked back or fooled around like the other kids, but, man, when he smiled the first time, it lit up his face completely. Stole my heart then and there. I've been watching him grow up ever since."

An unexpected—unwanted—spurt of longing shot through him. He scratched at the scruff itching his jaw, trying to get rid of the absurd emotion. He didn't want to have a special place in Reena Wells's heart. Learning more about her only confused and fed the annoying, deep impulses…like the one pushing him now. Don't ask—"Classes?" he asked despite himself.

"Yeah. I have one starting next weekend." She plucked a pine cone off the twig and fiddled with it. The bandages no longer protected her palms and the injuries looked angry and sore. "Twice a year I teach an art class at the community center. We meet on Saturdays, midmorning, for four weeks for an hour or two." Parts of the pine cone fell between her bent legs to float away with the water. "To keep it interesting and fresh, I change the mediums, so we could be water coloring one class then photographing the next."

"That's really cool." Nathan pictured her in front of an easel, showing students how to paint with sun radiating throughout the room. "How long have you been teaching?"

"About five years." She tossed the destroyed cone. "When I moved back home after college, I opened my art gallery. To help advertise the studio and stay in touch with the community, I began offering the classes." A new cone replaced the old. "My students range from middle-schoolers to retirees. That makes it fun."

"And Vincent?"

"He's got natural talent." Reena paused mangling the latest victim. "Vincent's father left a long time ago. His mother works two jobs to support them and rarely has money to spare. So, Vincent pays for my classes on his own." Half the cone plopped into the water. "I wish he'd let me waive the charge but he won't. After school, he rides his bike to the main tourist section of downtown and runs the cash register at a kitschy shop to earn money."

Nathan huffed a chuckle. "I wave the white flag. You don't have to sell me on him anymore." He pantomimed surrendering. "I like him. Okay? I admit it."

"Woohoo!"

Nathan snapped his face up. Ashleigh had her fists in the air while straddling the top of the trunk. She leaned against an upright branch with Vincent facing her, mimicking the pose. Wow. When had he stopped paying attention to the teens?

"Who won?" Reena shouted, then groaned under her breath.

"Tie," Ashleigh answered at the same time Vincent yelled, "I won."

"You did not!" Ashleigh's arms dropped.

"I had a backpack," Vincent countered. "That automatically makes my route tougher. Ergo, I won when you didn't arrive first."

"Oh boy." Reena tossed the destroyed pine cone to the side. "We're going to have to listen to this debate for hours."

Nathan's stomach squeezed. "Guess it's our turn to climb."

"Yep."

"Is it safe enough up there for you two to explore a bit?" Nathan yelled, wanting to prevent the teens from seeing Reena's pain. "Are the rock ledges wide enough to walk on? See if there's a better way down."

"I know what you're doing," Reena announced, leaning forward, breaking contact. "It chaps my pride, but thank you."

"I don't know what you're talking about," he lied, grabbing on to the limbs again. "I'm saving myself from endless teasing once my niece witnesses my humiliation."

"Great," Reena chirped. She resumed her crouched position. "That means I get to do it all."

"Oh, ha, ha." Nathan glanced at Reena's eviscerated gauze and winced. "Wait." He managed to swing his backpack around without falling off the branch and opened the large compartment. Leaning over to keep as much water out as possible, he grimaced as he reached inside. Dirtying everything in his search was low on his list of troubles, but it still bothered him. "Gotcha." He pulled out a pair of white socks, then rezipped the bag.

"What are you doing?" She eyed the socks with concern. "I don't think changing now is going to help anything."

"They're for your hands." He offered them to her.

Rain soaked into the cotton fabric as she stared at them.

Rolling his eyes, he attested, "They're clean." He shook them. "You need something to cushion your palms and this is all I've got."

"Oh." She slid them out of his fingers. "Good idea."

"So, how do we do this?" He studied the trial ahead, swallowing his pride at the question.

Reena finished adjusting the second sock over her wrist. Lifting her hands, she held them by her shoulders and made sock puppets. "To climb the branches, you want to walk like a dog." Her fingers moved in time with her words.

"Cute." And not distracting at all. "Wait. Did you say 'walk like a dog'?"

"Sure did." She grinned, her sock puppets now pantomiming laughter, he suspected at his skeptical face.

"Why?" Was she punking him?

"Because you need to distribute your weight evenly across your body or you'll lean too far to one side and fall."

"Ah." Made sense…sort of.

"When you step with your left foot, your right hand is moving up then vice versa." Thankfully, she stopped the puppet show. "You want to keep moving your hand and foot at the same time." She motioned to her left. "Move to that bunch."

He resituated his pack, then crab-walked awkwardly.

"Grab on to two branches close to your shoulder width when possible," she continued, showing him as she talked. "Since we don't have the luxury of rungs like the rope ladder, we have to use what we can for our footing."

Oh boy. He already did not like this. "Gotcha." Clearing his throat, he raised his butt and jammed his boots into a nest of branches tangled together. When they didn't loosen, he grabbed on to two limbs; one three inches, the other two inches thick, with lots of poky needle heads.

"Excellent." Reena reached forward with her left hand and clasped another section of her branch inches above. "See how my right foot is moving in time with my left hand placement?"

Now he got it. With all the grace of a newborn baby, he tried to imitate her. Wobbling and almost falling, he white-knuckled the limb to keep from going over.

"Don't overcorrect!" she snapped just as his hips went to counter his swing.

He slowed his body and exhaled at staying upright-ish.

"This is a lot harder than the game at the fair," Reena grunted. "Trust me. But we'll make it."

Seeing his socks protecting her hands, he wished he had donned a pair, too. Between the bark, needles, and pine cones, he'd be lucky if his palms didn't look like hers by the time he was through.

"Ready to try again?" Reena asked, peering at him.

"Absolutely." Not. He lifted his rickety right hand and left foot to try again.

Chapter Seventeen

Bark dug into Reena's forehead, probably leaving an impression behind, but she didn't care. She earned her reward for reaching the trunk. Resting against an upright branch, she dangled her legs over the tree. Agony speared her hips and thumped through every cell of her body. *Dear Lord, please make it stop.*

Thunder rumbled, gentling its ferocity as it rolled.

"If only I had my camera," Ashleigh wheezed, laughing so hard, she hugged a tall, vertical branch near the rock wall edge.

Reena's lips twitched and she tried valiantly to restrain a giggle, but it broke through her pain haze and flew free.

"You, too?" Nathan grumbled, pausing as he plucked pine cone bits and needles out of his hair. He was covered. Sitting sideways, facing the trail below they hadn't been able to see before, he scowled. "I could've been seriously hurt, you know."

"But you weren't, soooo," Ashleigh chortled, "that makes it *hilarious.*"

His expression flattened and he went back to plucking, his motions more pronounced than before.

"If it makes you feel any better—" Vincent held on to the same support as Ashleigh with one foot on the rock top "—I didn't think a squirrel would still be in the tree, either."

"It does not," Nathan muttered. "But thanks for still talking about it."

"Like we could stop," Reena answered, the mental video flaring in her head. "You should have seen your face when that squirrel popped his furry head through that clump."

Ashleigh threw her head back, howling. "Yeeesss!" She choked and slapped her chest. "I'm so glad we were here for the show." Inhaling deep, she pointed at her uncle. "You were already teetering so hard, I thought you'd bounce Reena out of the tree, then *bam!* Squirrel head."

Nathan yanked a twig from the collar of his shirt and hurled it.

Vincent shoved his face into his shoulder, his body quaking with silent laughter.

"I'm impressed by your vocal range," Reena gushed, then ruined it by snorting. "I never knew such a deep voice could hit a note that high."

Nathan's arm froze mid-throw with a pine cone chunk near his ear. "He was going for my heart!" He launched the cone so hard, he had to grab a branch or sail with it.

"Sure he was," Ashleigh scoffed, nodding really large. "I mean, everyone knows squirrels love chowing on human hearts."

"Squirt." Nathan glared at his niece.

She beamed. "I'm amazed at how fast you moved."

"Your reflexes are impressive." Vincent pantomimed jumping back.

"Don't bother sucking up if you're insulting me at the same time." Nathan tossed a clump of needle heads at the teens.

Reena hooked an elbow around her support and sat up. "I give your dismount a solid eight."

"But he deserves a ten for style." Ashleigh wiggled and glided her hands in front of her. "Managing to catch yourself on the set of limbs next to you...*upside down* deserves respect."

Nathan lowered his head, muttering something under his breath. "That stupid squirrel kept squeaking at me like *I* was the problem."

"Yeah." Reena nodded. "The whole time he darted away, he really was vocal."

"And let's talk about *your* style points, Reena." Ashleigh raised her hands and quacked her fingers and thumbs. "What's with the sock puppets?"

Reena studied the thick, athletic cotton blackened by the tree. "Your uncle's idea to cover the torn bandages. It worked."

The sky brightened with lightning and Reena flinched. "We need to move. I don't like being in the open. Especially this high."

"Oh, good." Nathan flapped his sopping T-shirt, detritus whipping away with the wind. "We're done picking on me."

"Not even close," Reena retorted. "We're just taking a break. I fear you'll never live this down."

"Peachy." He used the tall branch to help him gain his feet. Carefully weaving through the limbs like orange cones on a bike course, Nathan paused beside Reena and offered his hand.

Reena didn't hesitate or balk. She latched on. Between

his strength and the tree's limbs, she managed to stand, groaning the whole way. "What did you guys find?" She drew in small breaths to counter the cyclone of pain while peering at the teens.

"It's no good." Vincent pointed to the area ahead and behind him on the right side. "These trees and shrubs hide a drop-off so steep, it's almost a cliff that goes waaaaaaayyyyyyyy down."

"Same with that side." Ashleigh jabbed a finger to the left rock wall.

"Fresh tea." Reena sighed and ignored Nathan and Ashleigh's snicker at using their term. "I was afraid of that."

Thunder cracked.

"Time to go." Reena eyed their only way down. From up here, it looked like a looonnngg trip to the bottom.

"I say we slide," Vincent announced. "The branches are just as tight and tangled on this side and we'd be going in the same direction as the needles, not against them."

"Woot!" Ashleigh cried. "That's my kind of fun!"

"Uh." Nathan scratched the back of his neck. "You sure we wouldn't just bounce off the surface? I can see us flying in the air and splatting in the mud."

Reena bit her lip and calculated the risks. The spruce's needle clumps grew almost the entire length of the limb to the trunk. That gave them plenty of cushion and room to use. "I say we butt slide. Use our feet to help control our descent."

"All right!" Ashleigh scrabbled to sit near Reena. "We spreading out and going at the same time?"

"Good idea." Reena poked Nathan in the gut. "You've got to move closer to the rock wall, mister."

"You sure about this?" The corners of his eyes tightened and he divided his gaze between Ashleigh and the trail below. "The tree's not going to roll or anything with all our weight on one side, is it?"

"We're not going to be on it that long if we scoot." Reena pushed him gently. "Go."

"Ashleigh—"

"Will be fine."

Nathan shot one last look at his niece, then weaved toward the wall.

Once they were spread evenly, and sitting on the trunk with their feet enmeshed in the limbs, she gave the signal. "Go."

Barely controlled chaos ensued. The branch angle was just as steep as the other side; hair-raisingly vertical but not perpendicular.

Ashleigh and Vincent whooped and trash-talked as they raced down their designated sections.

"Ashleigh," Nathan barked. "Pay attention!"

Reena snapped her gaze off the greenery between her knees and gulped. Ashleigh was on her side, squealing with glee as she latched on to Vincent's sleeve. The two continued sliding, their feet completely off the tree.

A pine cone scratched up her outer thigh, catching on her spandex shorts before shearing away. She had to focus on her own descent. Using her arms and her boots, she tried to regulate herself, but it wasn't going well. Taking a page from the kids' book, she eased the pressure on her heels and allowed gravity to take over.

"Umph." A beat. "Ow!" Nathan growled, his slide picking up speed.

Limbs, clumps of needle heads, and pine cones dug into her body, and the branches were not smooth *at all*.

Mogul skiers were nuts if they enjoyed jarring their bones.

Her boots slammed onto the muddy trail, sending an impact all the way to her head. "Ice. Cold. Fresh. Tea." She flopped back, bouncing on the mass until it settled.

"That was awesome!" Ashleigh cheered. "I want to do it again."

Nathan jerked to a stop, his boots spraying mud as he landed hard. "I *never* want to do that again."

Keeping her eyes closed, Reena searched her brain for a silver lining to block out the pain. The only thing she could manage was that they had scaled a tree and no one broke a bone. Win.

Chapter Eighteen

"I ripped my shorts."

Reena's eyes popped open at that declaration. Rain instantly attacked her eyeballs.

Jerking upward, rubbing her abused eyes, Reena widened her feet to keep from falling forward. Dizziness fuzzed her mind and blurred her senses. She sat up way too fast.

Ashleigh burst out laughing. "Oh man. You did!"

Vincent twisted his upper half with impressive dexterity and glared at the frayed edges of a two-inch tear. Luckily, it was lower on his thighs than his butt. Hole or not, those shorts were stained beyond recovery.

"You needed to retire those raggedy things anyway." Reena planted her hands beside her and pushed to her feet.

"They're my favorite!"

"We can tell." Ashleigh snorted, dancing away from Vincent's attempted flick.

Reena made a mental note to buy him a new pair. Knowing her, she wouldn't wait until Christmas to give them to him. His birthday had already passed, so she had to invent a plausible reason. They weren't charity. Vincent worked so hard, and juggled so much, he deserved to be rewarded.

If they ever got off the mountain. The reasonable course of action would be to burrow until the storm passed. Earlier today she would've advocated for it, but she had to scrap the smart choice. With only two packs of supplies now sustaining four people, they couldn't afford the delay. And the way they were chewing up "daylight," she'd have to start hunting for an area to set up camp. Much sooner in the journey than she hoped.

"Let's go, troops." Reena stifled a moan taking her first step. Trees had it in for her today.

Mud splooshed and spattered beneath Nathan's tromps as he made his way to walk beside her. A small flutter in her belly had her rubbing the spot to make it go away. Reacting like a schoolgirl because an arresting man chose to spend time with her instead of his niece was ridiculous.

The water wasn't as prevalent on this side of the trail as the other. Rivulets still cut into the path and puddles reigned supreme, but they weren't wading through a newly made stream. The four of them fell into the same formation as earlier.

"Follow the yucky mud road," Ashleigh warbled off-key. She continued making up words to the song with her arm hooked around Vincent's elbow.

Reena had one year until she reached thirty, yet Mother Nature's beating made her feel ancient. Or was it Ashleigh's levity in spite of everything? Both, she decided.

"Squirt." Nathan peered over his hunched shoulder. "Improvising lyrics is not your strong suit."

"Neither is your singing," Vincent groaned, covering his hooded ears.

"Hey." Ashleigh pulled her arm free. "Just because you don't appreciate my genius—"

"Genius?" Vincent retorted, laughing. "You are many things, Ash, but a musical Einstein is not one of them."

"Just like you're not the winner." Ashleigh jabbed Vincent's biceps.

"Dream on," Vincent gloated. "I totally won…"

Reena tuned out the argument. Trekking between the high rock walls gave her something to concentrate on. The hobbling just added a flare to her trail walk. She inwardly shook her head.

"I'm not going to ask if you're okay," Nathan said in a lowered voice. "But are you good enough to keep going?"

"Of course," she automatically answered. "We can't stop now. It'll be too dark soon. We have to take advantage of the light." Shrubs lining the rock ledge above burst with the state's official flower, mountain laurel. The beautiful white and pink blossoms shook and danced with the rain and wind, making a mockery of the storm's gloominess.

Nathan rubbed the scruff on his jaw.

Thanks to the new awareness she totally did not want, she could tell he was mulling something in his mind. His musky scent carried in the gusts, surrounding her to the point she couldn't escape. If only she didn't find it so attractive. By now, the curiosity of Nathan Porter should have waned. But, no. She still couldn't stop thinking about him. The conversations they shared meant more because he kept everyone in Bell Edge on the other side of his wall, yet he shared with her. And his dedication to his niece hit her directly in the heart.

Alarm bells rang in the back of her mind and she heeded the warning. She had to stop. He had made it plain what he thought of her outlook on life—naive and irritating—and he showed no hint he harbored any interest in her beyond a guide off the mountain.

"I've noticed something about you, Ms. Sunshine." Nathan cut into her contemplation.

"And what's that?" She braced for another shot at her positive attitude.

"You put everyone else first," he announced bluntly.

Oh. Not what she expected. "Um—"

"That's admirable to a point."

She lifted her boot out of a puddle. "To a point," she repeated. "I'm sensing a 'but' coming." Because, of course, Nathan couldn't just say something nice without one.

He slid her a look, water dripping off his long eyelashes. "*But* you can't do that anymore."

She crossed her arms gingerly. Vulnerability rippled through her and she hated it. She was used to being healthy and independent. Not tenaciously independent to the point of idiocy, but able to stand on her own two feet without anyone wondering how. "When or if I need help, I'll ask for it."

"Sure you will." Nathan pointedly looked at a sock-covered hand. "Remind me. When did you ask for the first-aid kit?"

"I plead the Fifth." She jammed her hands into her coat pockets and studied the unchanging trail ahead with far more attention than it deserved.

Smug man. Just because he was right about her putting others first did not mean he could become her self-appointed watchdog. What if she preferred asking for Vincent's help? She didn't, much to her frustration, but shouldn't she have a choice as far as he knew? *See,* she crowed to her heart, *this is another reason why Nathan can't be my soul mate.* Pushy, know-it-all men didn't interest her in the least.

But a man who selflessly dives into danger to rescue you is *a candidate*, her heart shot back. Oh please. Hauling her away from the tree before they climbed wasn't a rescue. She was never in danger, but she understood the point. Nathan hadn't realized it at the time. He'd reacted to what he'd thought was imminent peril…and really, it wasn't out of the realm. She'd already been knocked down by one tree today and had another try to put her in traction.

Quiet descended over the group. Ashleigh gave up rewriting lyrics, Vincent hadn't said much anyway, and Nathan kept other observations to himself. For now.

The trail wound through the rock, leisurely twisting left and right. Her calves had a workout going up short, steep inclines then back down again all while avoiding rocks buried in the mud. Instead of stopping, they decided to munch on power bars and tip their heads back to drink the abundant rainwater. Ashleigh and Vincent took on the task of collecting rain in the water bottles they had finished earlier in order to stretch the meager supply. The unambiguous path allowed them to make up a little of the time they lost because of the blockade. She wanted to push harder but her injuries just wouldn't allow it.

With nothing much different in the scenery to occupy her, Reena let her mind wander. A free range of thoughts flitted through until she snagged one that interested her. Nathan. Of course. But not in the usual way. His complexity would be so interesting to capture on canvas. So many shades of brown were needed for his hair and jaw scruff, and definitely his eyes. Could she portray the seriousness mixing with the jewel he had in his arsenal, the spark of humor? She wasn't sure. His vast layers beneath the wall were deep and striking. His struggle and anger at God added to his complexity, and no portrait worthy of him could exist without these traits. If she didn't show them all, then she wouldn't do him justice.

The ultimate challenge gripped her so hard and so fast, ideas and techniques consumed her. Painting him rough and dirty in the midst of the forest intrigued her so much, her fingers twitched to grab her small sketch pad out of her backpack. She could see the portrait developing so clearly, it was like unveiling a photograph.

"What are you doing?"

Reena blinked at Nathan's question, the image receding but not disappearing completely. "What?"

"Your hands."

She snapped her gaze down and found her right arm raised and her fingers twitching within the sock, simulating sketching on her pad. "Oh. Ah." Mortification flooded her and she dropped her arm. No way was she telling *him* what she was doing. "Nothing."

His eyes narrowed and he hummed. "Nothing." He nodded. "Sure. That's totally normal behavior."

"It is for an artist," she retorted, bristling at his *you're crazy-toons* tone.

"Aha!" he crowed. "So, you were doing something."

"Yes, Mr. Nosy." Reena lifted her chin, brazening it out. "An idea for a painting came to mind and I guess I was working through it." Visually. Like a crazy-toons.

"Oh yeah?" His features lightened and he tilted his head. "What's it about? Er, or do you say 'what's the subject'?" His fingers combed through his hair, leaving waves until the rain flattened them again. "I don't know art terms."

Why did she have to find his fluster so darn cute? "You got it right the second time," she answered, not telling him he should've asked "who" the subject was in this case. Scrabbling to come up with something plausible, she scratched her nose. "Just a scene on the mountain."

"Like random trees and rocks?" Nathan snorted, waving a hand in front of him. "And unrelenting rain?"

She chuckled weakly. She didn't want to lie but just the thought of admitting *he* was the subject... No. Way. Jose. "It's just starting to form in my mind, but it will have trees and maybe rocks. Not sure about the rain."

Nathan's boots slurped out of the mud. "There's certainly been plenty. I don't understand the appeal of camping or hiking in the forest."

"That's because you've only seen it during a storm," Reena replied, relieved he had steered the subject away from the painting. "It's really breathtaking normally. Especially when the sun illuminates lush green foliage in the summer or riotous colors in the fall. Multistory-tall waterfalls and rugged landscapes drive home how small humans really are."

"Are you comparing it to what people say about the ocean when they stand in front of it?"

"Exactly." Reena dodged around a deep rivulet, brushing against the rock wall as it curved left. "They're both humbling and majestic."

"I love the mountains *and* the ocean," Ashleigh inserted, closer behind them than before.

"Me, too," Vincent chimed in. "Although, I think Ash just likes getting a tan on the beach."

"I can think deep thoughts and soak up the sun at the same time," Ashleigh retorted.

"Deep thoughts like should I flip over or what's for dinner?" Vincent joked, moving out of Ashleigh's arm range.

The trail's curve ended and a vast view opened before them.

Chapter Nineteen

Nathan blinked and halted. After hiking between the tall stone walls and towering trees for so long, the sudden openness caught him by surprise. Maneuvering to the corner of the rock wall, he placed a palm against the slimy lichen/moss. The strong, dank tang pinched his nostrils.

Hot gusts of wind slammed into him, forcing him to tighten his grip as the rain lashed against him, no longer filtered through a canopy—and that was miserable before. "Wow, it's harsh up here."

"But so vast," Ashleigh breathed, her voice barely carrying to his ears.

Nathan laced his fingers together, holding them above his eyes like a visor. Ohhhh. A river valley lay below them. So many different types of dense, lavish trees in varying shades of green climbed the other side to form another mountain face. Occasional open lines squiggled through the canopies and vegetation. Ravines? Gorges? Or was that saying the same thing? He felt so out of his element.

They had come out near a peak. He couldn't tell if the

top was pointed like typical mountain pictures, but he figured it was probably similar to the rounded shape the other side sported. Instead of a forest filling the land on their side, boulders, lines of rocks, and deadfalls jutted from the wild meadow slanting downward. Seriously downward. Like only the most psychotic adventure junkie would want to sled or ski down its angle—setting aside the body-breaking obstacles, of course. Tall, wide blades of grass ruffled in the wind in waves with clumps of shrubs fighting for natural light; he bet in the spring it all flowered and blazed like a rainbow in the sun.

Wow. Now he sounded like Reena. In this instance, he'd admit it wasn't a bad way to imagine the valley below.

Carrying on the wind, ozone enhanced the rich aroma of the varied vegetation. It was overwhelming but pleasant.

"I've never been here before," Vincent announced, standing between the other rock wall and Ashleigh.

"You know I haven't." Ashleigh wiped her face with her wet sleeve.

"Neither have I." Reena flattened a hand over her eyebrows, the blackened sock standing out against the yellow coat. "It sure is amazing. I wish it wasn't raining. I bet it's stunning."

"Uh." Nathan slowly straightened, his stomach lowering at the same speed. "What now? You've never been here?" He swished his hand toward the valley. "You planned this weekend. How is that possible?"

Reena's arm dropped and she frowned at Nathan. "Our hike didn't include this section of the mountain."

"So you have no clue what type of terrain exists or what we're up against?" His stomach settled in his foot.

"No." She faced him directly.

"But…" He grappled with the implications. "You've lived here your whole life, right?"

"These aren't the local trails around Bell Edge. You remember driving an hour, right? Do you know how huge the Pocono Mountains are?" She pierced him with hazel irises starting to spark. "They stretch over four counties and are part of the Appalachian Mountain system. If you're unfamiliar with how vast the Appalachians are, *they* range from southeast Canada to Alabama." A socked finger poked her own chest. "I've explored quite a bit, but there is no way I could hike *every* trail."

Moisture fled Nathan's mouth and his stomach roiled. He had been counting on Reena's expertise, her knowledge of the area. "Then how do you know about the trail splitting and where they'll lead?"

"I studied maps when I planned the weekend." She adjusted her hips, trying to hide a grimace, but he caught it. "I specifically planned a route that kept us on the benign side of the mountain. We were never supposed to cross the bridge, but it happened. We're now forced to traverse the trails meant for advanced hikers."

The words rang in his ears like ominous gongs.

"I don't remember every single detail since I didn't study this side that hard." She continued firing at him. "But we're heading toward where we can signal for help."

Heat wrapped around his hand, startling him. He glanced over to find Ashleigh clasping his palm between hers. "I'm sorry, Uncle Nathan."

Nathan closed his eyes. *Way to go.* He had just broadcast his fears and doubts, undermining his role as the all-knowing, unfazed protector. Kissing Ashleigh's wet forehead, he murmured against her skin, "I know you are." He had to get it together. Pulling back, he bluffed confidence. "Awesome. It'll be refreshing to know I'm not the only one who has no clue what's coming."

"Way to find a silver lining." Reena grinned, her eyes sparkling.

He had to admire the five-foot-three ball of eternal happiness, but he had to stop the gravity constantly pulling him toward her. Once they escaped the mountain, he had to focus on establishing the new hub of his company in Bell Edge and raising Ashleigh. Instilling his niece with common sense and the importance of weighing decisions carefully *before* acting became a number-one priority, and Reena's adventurous spirit would sabotage those lessons. Whoa. He shouldn't even be thinking about Reena having an influence on Ashleigh's upbringing. A relationship with Reena…he couldn't see it working. Yet, even as he protested, a part of him could. And *that* alarmed him.

Nathan shut down his thoughts and perused the landscape. The right side of the rock wall continued. Jagged edges covered in moss and vines rose even higher, forming a cliff face. The left wall ended with giant boulders lying in pieces, allowing enough space for a single line of people to pass by.

Reena took the lead and maneuvered around an oval boulder. Only then did Nathan notice large flattish stones in the ground acting like stairs. Dirt and undergrowth claimed the space between, making them treacherous to walk on. Waiting until Ashleigh and Vincent fell in line behind Reena, he took his first step on the uneven surface. His boots landed on the top stone with a thud and the wind hurled against him. Thankfully, the path didn't lead straight down—that'd be leg-breaking for sure. It cut across the rocky meadow as it descended.

Thunder resounded, echoing louder than before.

Reena flinched, slapping her palm against the rock wall and ducking her head.

Nathan didn't blame her. Having the cover of trees had given him a false sense of security. Even though Reena had been the victim of lightning striking a tree, out here there was nothing between him and the clouds. If lightning struck, one of them could be its target. Maybe they should have made a shelter out of the downed evergreen instead of scaling it. He wanted to get Ashleigh home, no doubt, but was it smart to keep going?

Small streams of water cut across the stones and rushed to burrow into the wild landscape. The undergrowth bobbed in its force and the dirt had long since become slippery mud.

The weight of his backpack cut into his shoulders and he longed for a break. He wasn't used to hefting something on his back for this long, let alone fighting it against the elements. The pack shifted off-center, throwing his weight toward the open, plunging slope.

A strange silence swamped the area then a chilling crack boomed. The ground shook violently and Nathan flung his arms up as his boot slid off the stone.

"MUDSL—"

The earth dropped out from beneath Nathan and he plummeted downward.

Chapter Twenty

~❦~

"Mudslide!" Reena screamed, desperately clinging to the rock wall, the ground shaking like an earthquake. *"Run!"*

Ashleigh and Vincent took off, running so fast they almost hit her. Reena flattened as small as she could and yelled, *"Go around me!"*

The teens listened and bolted.

Reena's heart pounded so hard, she couldn't breathe. They had to clear the area. Mudslides were unpredictable. They could flow a few feet wide to encompassing a whole side of a mountain. The summer version of an avalanche.

The only saving grace they had right now was the stone-laden path cut alongside the cliff face instead of carving straight down into the ravine.

Hips screaming and muscles locking, Reena clamored as fast as she could.

"Uncle! Nathan!"

Ashleigh's wail froze the blood in Reena's veins. She whirled and found…nothing. No sign of Nathan.

A sob tore Reena's throat and she howled, *"Nathan!"*

Wildly searching, her gaze barely comprehended anything. *"Nathan!"*

A river of mud whooshed down the slope, the force growing more powerful every second. Clutching the rock wall, she scanned the flow and spied touches of skin poking among the mud.

Oh no. Oh no. Oh no. Oh. No.

The roar of the landslide muted everything.

"Nathan!" she bellowed. He probably couldn't hear her, but she couldn't stop calling his name.

"He's in the mudslide," Ashleigh screamed, fighting against Vincent's hold. *"Let me go!"*

Reena found the teens a quarter mile down the stone trail, clear of the immediate danger. The mudslide hadn't expanded wider.

Terror clogged her thoughts and she couldn't decide what to do. Keep the teens safe here or go after Nathan. Before she knew she had made a decision, her boots were stomping down the path. Ignoring her injured hips and body, she ran. Recklessly. Stupidly. She kept charging. Lopsided surfaces snagged her tread, pushing her off-balance, but she wouldn't stop.

Vincent clamped Ashleigh tight around her arms and chest, wrestling her against the wall. Reena turned sideways and stuttered past, Ashleigh stilling only when Reena was beside them.

"Put me down!" Ashleigh demanded.

Reena didn't slow or bother looking. Vincent would either do what the girl said or not. They were safe. Nathan was…her heart exploded with fear.

The stone and dirt path continued its angled descent, but in one direction. No switchback. Nathan was the other way. By the time she reached the bottom, who knew how far away she'd end up? But did she dare cross the meadow? The vegetation was so tall, it hid a lot more obstacles than the boulders she could see—

"No!" Vincent barked. "Ash, stop!"

Reena slowed her frantic pace in time to see Ashleigh jump off a path into the tall grass. The blades covered most her legs, showing only the tops of her thighs and up.

The teen's impulsive decision made Reena's easier. Surging off the stone, she dropped into greenery. The furious roar of the mudslide drilled into her skull, egging her on. Lightning flashed, sticks spanning the sky, and she ducked, the response automatic. Nothing protected her from its vengeance in the open. Adrenaline choked her and she gagged against so much terror coursing through her.

Her hips keened at her jostling and seized.

Nathan. *Dear Lord, please, please, please,* she prayed, unable to articulate her need. Crying out at the agony, she stumbled. *Go, Reena.* She did. Running in the meadow was an act of faith and constant prayer. Her boots kept tangling with the vines and limbs wrapping around her feet and ankles. To her left, a red rain-coated streak caught up to the blue-and-black-clad figure struggling to climb over a giant rock. Reena didn't have the luxury of someone watching over her. Her self-appointed watchdog…another sob caught in her throat. Nathan needed *her* to help him this time and she couldn't let him down.

Forcing her boot forward, she ripped the patch of wintercreeper vines out of the ground. The torrential rain had made the landscape so slippery, twice she almost body-surfed down the slope. If she knew what lay at the bottom, she'd go for it, but the land dipped out of sight, hiding the lower half. She only knew a river existed, not what type of terrain lined the banks. Could be tall boulders or it could be soft foliage.

Her stomach roiled. Nathan. What had Nathan landed on or against?

The mudslide ceased pouring from the top of the mountain. The last of the frenzied water carried branches and small rocks with it as it continued its destructive path. Behind, it left a swath of uprooted plants and mud with only the craggy boulders and fresh deadfall standing strong.

Every cell in her body cried in anguish. She couldn't keep up this pace. She couldn't stop, either.

"I have to find him," Ashleigh wailed, her voice carrying on the unforgiving wind. "I can't lose him, too."

Tears poured out of Reena's eyes, mixing with the rain on her face. *Dear Lord, help her.* What the fifteen-year-old must be going through.

"I did this, Vincent," Ashleigh continued, her babbling morphing into a confession. "It's all my fault."

"He's okay, Ash." Vincent balanced her hand while she scrabbled over an oblong rock, his eyes full of worry.

"You don't know that."

No, they didn't. Reena could only hope Vincent's words proved true.

"Look." Ashleigh pointed at the destruction left behind. "He was in that."

"I know." He yelped and disappeared.

"Vincent?" Reena shouted, stumbling on moldering branch limb.

"I'm fine." He popped up. "Hole." He pointed down. "Watch out."

Reena castigated herself for running headlong into the meadow. Vincent could've broken a leg just then.

Not to mention tangled with whatever animal dug that hole for its home.

"Why did I insist on swimming?" Ashleigh's pace picked up. She no longer heeded the danger, she flat out ran. *"Uncle Nathan!"*

It reminded Reena of how Nathan acted when he dashed after Ashleigh. The Porters were consistent.

"Ashleigh!" Vincent tore after her.

Reena chased after them both. She could not let anything happen to either of them. Yet, finding Nathan drove her the hardest.

Wild shrubs, once beautiful, turned into hurdles. She couldn't jump over their height, so she barreled through them. And they fought back. Smacking into anything they could reach, she bore scratches and cuts.

Uh! Her body lunged forward in her run but her left foot remained behind. Unable to stop the momentum, she slammed into the ground, the greenery cushioning her fall only so much. Two inches to the right, she spied a spiky stone that would've smashed her face. This was insanity. She had to slow down.

She had to help Nathan.

Tearing at the wintercreeper vine wrapped around her ankle, she tugged hard. Facing the top of the mountain, she wrenched her leg to the side at the same time she heaved. The vine snapped free, swinging her leg uncontrollably. Dragging her with it, she toppled over, then couldn't stop. The steep angle took over and rolled her sideways. She frantically threw her arms out, clutching at anything to stop her descent. Images of impaling her body on a sharp rock consumed her.

No. No. No. Blades of grass whipped through her sock-covered hands and varied shrubs tore at the roots. Her speed increased, tossing her off-balance, rolling her over her shoulder. Scrabbling with everything she had, she kept clawing—

And snagged a honeysuckle vine.

Ice. Cold. Fresh. Tea. Her body slammed to a halt, pain sliced through her shoulder socket.

Dropping her forehead to the ground, she panted and whimpered. Pooling rain sprayed up her nose and she sneezed, adjusting her head to lay on her still straight arm.

Thank you, Lord. Closing her eyes, she forced herself to just breathe. Too much agony competed for her attention and she wasn't sure if her legs could support her right now.

"Reena!" Vincent shouted, making her wince.

Rest time was over. Grabbing her temple with her free hand, she yelled, "I'm okay." *Ugggghhh.* Her head pounded. Twisting her wrist back and forth, she worked free of the vine. Her skin covered in red whelps, she pulled the top of the sock down as far as it would go to hide them.

Standing was a testament to willpower. She could not let Nathan down.

Turning to search for the teens, she froze. Five more feet and she would have sailed over the edge of a small cliff.

Chapter Twenty-One

"Uncle Nathan!" Ashleigh screamed.

Reena focused on what lay below the twenty-foot drop. As she predicted, a river cut through the landscape, raging in the storm. Its banks swelled fat with water, devouring rocks and plants equally.

"I need to get down there," Ashleigh demanded. "I have to find him."

"We will." Reena scanned the cliff top. There had to be a way down. Below, the ground took on a rockier terrain with intermittent tufts of grass, sloping gently toward the river. Honeysuckle vines dominated the rock wall and top, their elongated white flowers waving in the wind and rain, leaving only a two-foot-wide path to the water. The sweet, citrusy fragrance clouded the air, overpowering the fresh smell of rain and the river.

"There." Vincent pointed to his right.

Reena ran to the small space carved into the vegetation, meeting the teens at the same time. Cut into the cliff was a makeshift staircase made of scarred, thick branch sections. She didn't hesitate. Her foot almost flew off the round log, its surface slimy and wet, but she latched on to the honeysuckles to stay upright. The steps descended almost straight down like a ladder. She should have faced the other way before she'd started, but she couldn't do anything about it now. Her body hurt too much to twist into a new position.

Scrabbling directly behind her told her the teens hadn't waited for her to clear.

Sinking into the mud, Reena shuffled to the side, over the small rocks and pebbles. *"Nathan!"*

Nothing. Her blood pressure skyrocketed and she clamped a hand over her heart in an attempt to keep the organ from leaping out of her chest.

The mudslide's destructive path laid waste to a massive swath of the landscape, easy to see from their position below. She didn't care. Frantically searching for any sign of Nathan on their level commanded her attention.

"Uncle Nathan!" Ashleigh started running toward the remains of the mudslide. It still oozed, spreading thinner as it sank into the river and found no resistance to claim the banks.

Reena caught up to the girl and grabbed her sleeve. "Slow down." Panting, she blinked against the black spots crowding her vision. "You don't want to get sucked in."

"But he's in there." Ashleigh yanked hard, ripping her coat from Reena's hold. "What if he's drowning?"

"We have to stay positive." Reena choked on the words. They tasted like ash and hopeful dreams. "He's fine." He had to be.

In two determined strides, Reena reached the river and glared at the jutting large sections of tree trunks, dead limbs, and mud seeping among its depths. Tears fell freely, half for Nathan and half for herself. Her body couldn't take much more, but she wouldn't stop until she found him. Hopping onto a boulder closest to the mudflow, she wobbled, her caked boots finding no traction on the wet surface. Like Pride Rock in *The Lion King*, the stone angled upward and she carefully moved to the end jutting over the water, then knelt and gripped the rough edge. "Come on, Nathan," she whispered, the socks on her hands another reminder of him. "Where are you?"

On the other side of the river, along a copse of virile shrubs, a large blob of mud wavered, a bubble forming. The murky dome rose high and thick. Reena sucked in a breath. Was that him? The mud shifted again, popping the bubble with a splat. The spark of hope fizzled.

"Do you see him?" Ashleigh asked, kneeling next to her. The teen erratically studied the area. Tears coursed down her cheeks and Reena's heart broke all over again.

A groan flitted over the storm, gripping Reena tight. Could it be?

Clutching the bottom of her throat, she vainly searched for the source.

"Did you hear that?" Ashleigh leaned farther over the rock. "I heard something."

Reena's lungs froze and she willed the sound to repeat itself.

It did.

"There it is again!" Ashleigh cried, clinging to Reena's forearm. "You heard it, too, right?"

Deep-chested coughing started then cut off with garbled hacking. "Uncle Nathan!" Ashleigh bolted to her feet, pivoting left and right. "Where are you? Are you okay? Why can't I see you? Vincent, Reena, do you see him?"

Reena strained her sight, searching, but she found nothing.

Nathan groaned again, long and deep.

Where was he?

"Uncle Nathan!" Ashleigh blasted.

Mud slurping and wet slapping echoed beneath Reena's ear.

She tilted her head—was he…? She carefully leaned forward. Hanging the top part of her body upside down, she peered underneath the upturned rock. Blood rushed to her head, not helping with her vision problem, but she squinted to decipher the dark shadows.

The darkness shifted, slowly edging away from the mudslide side.

"Nathan!" Elation blacked out Reena's vision and she pulled back, her forehead thudding the back of her hand. Bursting into a new round of tears, she let it all out, needing the outlet to calm down. *Thank you, Lord.* Nathan was alive.

Wretched hacking with intermittent gagging spits cut through Reena's breakdown. He needed help. "He needs help," she wheezed. A loud splash echoed.

"Uncle Nathan, I see you."

Vincent jumped off the rock and ran to Ashleigh's side, positioning himself to take the brunt of the river's fury. Chivalry remained alive with that boy. Pride touched her heart. She hoped he never changed.

Reena pushed herself upright, closing her eyes against the flashes of light and her woozy head. Her wrenched shoulder ached and her arms shook. With too much effort, she slowly wiggled until she lay flat against the rock. The teens waded farther into the river, the water crashing up their stomachs.

"Be gentle," Nathan croaked. "Having…trouble… catching my…breath."

More splashing filled the air and Reena rolled to the side edge of the rock farthest away from the mudslide. She blinked at first, unsure if her tear-filled eyes were playing tricks on her. But, no. The fern at the basin of the rock only had an inch of leaves showing. When she first climbed, it had been visible.

Then it hit her. She bolted upright, whirling. The mudslide continued feeding into the river. The rocks, dead trees, and detritus from the mudslide had crossed the entire width, forming a dam.

"Nathan! Ashleigh! Vincent!" Reena scrabbled to her feet, her body threatening to give out. "You have to get out from under the rock."

"We're trying," Vincent answered.

"I mean it," Reena barked. "The river's rising. You'll drown."

She trudged down the rock as fast as the slippery surface allowed and hopped onto the pebbled bank. The river churned and swirled, beating against the freshly formed barrier. Small waves crested on top to soak into the surface.

Ashleigh and Vincent guided Nathan from beneath the rock. His face plunked into the river and he jerked up, coughing.

"You guys trying to drown me?" He wheezed, mud sliding off his head in globs.

The teens struggled to help Nathan stand relatively straight. He weaved and blinked furiously. Scrubbing his face, he dashed the water over his hair.

Mud coated large sections where the river hadn't touched. Rips flapped open in his T-shirt and his shorts were torn. But he was standing. Talking. And relatively healthy…outside of the probable concussion.

Covering her mouth, Reena trembled and just allowed the tears to run free. Later, she'd analyze her insane actions, but for now she concentrated on not passing out.

Chapter Twenty-Two

Nathan had trouble holding on to a thought. His mind twirled and buzzed with a vengeance—

Ashleigh slammed into him. "I thought I lost you."

Losing his balance, he tipped over backward, splatting against the water. The backpack took the brunt but dragged him under the surface, or maybe it was Ashleigh bearing down on him. Or both. Either way, he sank.

Ashleigh shrieked and flailed, striking him in ways he'd surely feel later. Wrenching sideways, he planted a palm onto a rock and sat up. An impact to the top of his skull rattled his already fuzzy brain.

"Ow!" Ashleigh cried.

Nathan blinked at the water dripping past his eyes and spied his niece rubbing her chin. "Sorry."

"Me, too!" Her arms and legs wrapped around his body and she burrowed her face into his neck.

A violent tremor racked her and she broke down completely. The only other time he'd seen her cry like this was when her father died.

"I'm okay, squirt," he soothed, unable to control the slur. He bear-hugged her, the monkey clinging for all she was worth. His lungs were still on fire and he had an urge to keep hacking, but he refrained. Ashleigh needed him to be strong. Resting his forehead on her shoulder, he stroked her back and allowed his own tears to flow.

When her sobs quieted, he blurted the first thing he could think of to show he was fine. "Roller coasters have nothing on that trip down the mountain."

"You hate roller coasters."

"I'm rethinking that." The water swirled around him and he found himself rocking with it. "They've got to be a lot safer than a nature hike."

Ashleigh pulled back, offering him a wobbly smile. Her eyes were red-rimmed, her cheeks puffy, and who knew what happened to make her hair nest like that... she was beautiful and his heart overflowed.

"Love you, squirt." He kissed her cheek. "Up." He lightly smacked her thigh. "I'm getting wet."

A peal of glee lit her expression. "You are such a nerd."

"Runs in the family. Remember that."

With a dexterity he never possessed, Ashleigh rose in one fluid motion. A hand appeared in front of his face and he looked up the length of the arm. "Vinnie!" popped out before he thought about it. His jostled brain was having trouble connecting the dots.

The teen shook his head, his lips twitching the whole time. "Need help?"

"Is that a philosophical question or literal?" Uncaring the answer, he worked with the kid to stand. He peered down his length. "River dunking cleaned me off. Cool."

"Total nerd." Ashleigh swiped her hair, grimacing when she reached the worst of the snarl.

"It's funny," Nathan mused, going with the chaotic flow of his thinking. "When I turned twenty-one, Scott had taken me and some friends out to celebrate. I thought I had gotten beyond drunk then." He recalled all the shots and beer. "I mean my hangover lasted *three* days, but now?" He clutched his forehead. "I—"

A giggle caught his attention. Peering at Ashleigh, a grin spread his lips. "Oops. I'm not supposed to be telling those kinds of stories, am I?"

"I'm not stopping you," Ashleigh encouraged. "It's fascinating and educational."

He laughed. "Nope. Not getting me in trouble, squirt."

Movement out of the corner of his eye had him pivoting—well, stumbling in that direction. "Reena." His heart jolted and thumped *hard.* A thrill rushed through his veins, warming him deep inside. Reena Wells. Beautiful inside and out—

"Whoa, Ms. Sunshine." His brain caught up to his vision. "Did you go to war with the mountain?"

Her hood was down and long stalks of grass and twigs tangled throughout her hair, and stains covered her neon-yellow jacket. Mud caked her skin and her boots reminded him of the camouflage the military used to hide in the wilderness.

An image of a Reena-style warrior princess fascinated him. "That's very bloodthirsty and unlike you. I like it."

She ducked her head and wiped her cheeks.

"Wait." He sloshed forward, fighting against the current. "Are you…crying?" Finally reaching the edge, he stomped through the fern blocking his way and scrunched on pebbles and stones. "I know there's no crying in baseball, but is there crying in ultimate nature walks?"

"Ultimate nature walks?" Reena repeated, her voice strained and warbled.

"You know, like ultimate tag, just with trees and stuff

out to annihilate you." Nathan stopped in front of her. He no longer smelled strawberries and the disappointment surprised him. He missed the smell he now associated with her. Instead, he inhaled a mishmash of wet, wholesome nature. Using the side of his forefinger, he lifted her chin. She fought at first, then allowed him to win. Similar to his niece, Reena's cheeks were puffy and so much pain swam in her normally bright hazel eyes.

"Hey," he said softly, her sadness dousing his mirth. It was hard to get his brain to focus beyond a few seconds, but he tried anyway.

She swiveled her chin off his finger and added space between them. Both physically and emotionally. He could practically see a wall going up.

A feeling of loss pierced his heart. He didn't like the withdrawal…no. That wasn't right, was it? Something hummed at the edge of his awareness. He wanted the space? Yes. That was it. He didn't want to keep getting closer to Reena. Collecting pieces of her confused him and messed with the plan he had for the future. Those thoughts sounded right but felt wrong. The peace and warmth filling him when he was with her couldn't be an accident or a fluke. It meant something deeper, but what…? His line of thought floated away.

Reena cleared her throat. "How are you feeling besides concussed?"

"No broken bones as far as I can tell." He swished his hand. "Now, back to you. What happened? You look ready to pass out."

"Nothing." She blushed and shrugged.

He impatiently shifted his feet. "Stop being evasive."

"I'm not." Her chin jutted. "There's nothing to tell.

When we realized you were gone, we chased after you. End of explanation."

Liar, his instincts shot back. She was dodging the question, but why? If he could think clearly, he could probably figure it out.

Reena motioned to the narrowing span of space. "We need to move or we'll be walking through the water."

The overflowing river claimed more ground than he realized. The backs of his heels were disappearing within.

"Hold up." Ashleigh tugged on the bottom of his backpack. "Where's your tent?"

Twisting, he tried to look, but like a dog chasing his tail, the bag kept moving out of sight.

"I can't believe your pack survived that ride," Vincent commented, tugging on his own straps. "That's a commercial in the making right there."

"Maybe I'll make some money." Nathan held his dizzy and aching head. "I thought the salesman in the store was upselling me. Guess he knew what he was talking about after all." Nathan patted the side. "Hey." He felt both sides. "I lost my water bottle and sunglasses. *Maaannn.* I loved those glasses." All of a sudden, he clutched his stomach. "Uhhhhh. I feel sick." He made it as far as the other side of the rock before he lost his power bar.

A white, square wipe appeared. Still bent, he leaned one hand against the rock and took it. "Thanks." Scrubbing his face, he spit as much as he could to clear his mouth. "I feel like sleeping for the next twelve years." His eyelids were so heavy, he gave up trying to keep them open.

"Concussion." Reena's feminine voice soothed him and he wanted her to speak more.

"Is he going to be okay?" Ashleigh asked, worry lacing her tone.

"Yes, but we'll have to watch him," Thankfully, Reena answered, because he didn't feel up to it. All the weird euphoria mixed with the power bar leaving him in a vacuum of hurt.

The infernal rain pounding on his head increased his misery. "Is this storm ever going to end?" He groaned, easing upward and plopping a hip on the rock.

"It's already heading out," Reena answered.

"Could've fooled me," he muttered, rubbing the back of his neck with the wipe. "The humidity is unbearable."

"I'm hoping it'll lessen when the rain stops."

A warm palm spread over his forehead and he leaned into the soft touch. "Uncle Nathan, you don't feel feverish."

"Good to know." He pulled away from Ashleigh's palm and groaned. "I probably don't feel a tenth of what you do, Ms. Sunshine, but, wow. You are amazing for carrying on."

Reena shuffled her feet, the tips of her ears growing pinker by the second. "I don't know about all that, but thanks." She cleared her throat. "Do you want to change?" She motioned to his clothes.

His hand instantly rubbed down the front of his T-shirt. Rips and tears in varying lengths ruined his favorite shirt. He'd owned the hunter green tee with a defunct company's logo for years. His ripped shorts hadn't fared much better, but at least they held in the important parts.

"Nah." He shrugged, dropping his hand. "No sense destroying other clothing when I'm doing so well murdering these."

"I found it!" Vincent yelled.

Nathan searched for the teen and located Vincent partway up the slope he had slid down. Mud and water sloshed off the bright blue nylon housing the tent inside.

"It's kinda bent," Vincent shouted, picking his way through the thigh-high flora.

"Of course it is," Nathan muttered. Nothing about this weekend had gone right. Reena's bright yellow coat snagged his attention. More like Reena herself snagged his awareness. As usual. Maybe he'd gotten more out of this weekend than he'd bargained for, but that sentiment could be interpreted two ways. Maybe, just maybe, he should follow Reena's example. Before today, he'd grumble about God conspiring against him and list every negative thing that happened as proof. He still had a lot of anger, but at this moment, he was alive and relatively unhurt. God still had a lot to answer for in taking Scott too soon, but if He hadn't, Nathan would never have spent this time with Reena or become so much closer to Ashleigh.

He had a lot to think about and suddenly he didn't feel like punching a wall or dragging an anvil of anguish with every step.

Chapter Twenty-Three

Reena longed to stretch out and sleep for days. She honestly didn't know how she'd managed to stand for this long. Swaying with the wind, she swallowed against the gorge rising up her throat. There wasn't an inch that didn't throb, slice, or burn with pain.

"We getting out of here?"

She snapped her eyes open at Vincent's question. Peering up, she found him on top of the cliff, near the mudslide destruction swath. Tucked under an arm, he carried Nathan's tent as he paced the edge. The urge to break down and cry again tempted her hard. She couldn't go on. Physically, her body had hit its limit. The little bit of health it had retained after the tree incident, she'd destroyed with her demented run through the wild meadow. Mentally, she didn't know how much more she could take. Nothing had gone right since she'd sent the kids on the scavenger hunt.

Two thin arms carefully wrapped around Reena from behind and Ashleigh rested her chin on Reena's shoulder. "You may be our hotshot teen director, but I can totally take charge. You and Uncle Nathan just hang back, limp together, and signal if one of you is about to fall over. I got this."

"*We* got this," Vincent corrected, grinning. "Ash and I totally know what we're doing. Don't worry about a thing."

The ludicrous proposal was just what Reena needed. Laughter bubbled, shattering the depression and hopelessness taking hold.

"Is it just me, Reena—" Nathan gingerly rose from the rock "—or does their suggestion scare you?"

"Hey." Ashleigh lifted her chin. "Just because we have no idea where we're going, shouldn't count against us."

"Yeah." Vincent pointed skyward. "We'll use the sun to guide us."

A snort escaped Reena and she let the laughter run free.

"We go that way, right?" Ashleigh let go of Reena and swished an arm in the direction they had been heading when the mudslide hit.

"See?" Vincent nodded enthusiastically. "We're already ruling navigation."

"Oh boy." Nathan shuffled closer to Reena. "It's getting as deep as the water down here."

Nathan was right. The churning river had claimed more of the ground.

"I love you two," Reena answered, rallying her willpower. "And your offer is appreciated, but I'll keep leading."

"Aw, man," Ashleigh whined, exaggerating her disappointment. "I wanted to find a waterfall to ride next." She jutted a hip. "I mean you played with lightning, we all scaled a tree, and Uncle Nathan surfed a mudslide. Waterfall riding just has to be next."

A shudder rippled through Reena.

Nathan shifted as if fighting his own tremor at the

prediction. "The way this trip is going, it could happen." He shoved the wipe into the cargo pocket near his knee that couldn't close anymore thanks to the ripped flap. "At that point, y'all would definitely see a grown man cry."

"Oh, Uncle Nathan." Ashleigh patted his shoulder. "You don't have to pretend with me. Dad told me how you cried when the Nationals won the World Series."

"It was the first time DC won the championship since nineteen twenty-four," Nathan shot back, his shoulders hiking higher and his stance defensive. "I had season tickets. I was *invested*."

"I get it." Vincent shot finger guns at Nathan. "I felt the same when the Phillies won the World Series."

Reena rolled her eyes. "I was happy about the Phillies, but I didn't cry."

"Because you weren't invested," Nathan retorted, crossing his arms.

Seeing a losing argument, Reena went to put her hood up, but it got caught on… She felt the top of her head. Pulling on a long stalk, she found a piece of privet shrub still full of leaves. Great. Bet she took top prize in looking the most tragic. *Yay!* A girl dreamed of winning that when in the company of a captivating man.

No, Reena. She slammed the door closed on that thought. Her kamikaze race down the mountain really put her growing feelings in perspective. Nathan Porter wanted nothing to do with her emotionally, yet she'd almost killed herself to find him. She had to pull back and evaluate what she was doing or, more important, figure out why her soul latched on to the complex man. Treating him like a regular chaperone was the smart and competent thing to do from now on.

"Vincent, stay up there," Reena instructed, dropping

the last of the debris from her hair…or what she could feel was the last anyway. "We'll join you."

Swallowing the groan from her rebelling muscles, she began trudging toward the break in the thick honeysuckle. Their sweet, citrusy scent helped keep her focused and brought a nostalgic touch. Every time she inhaled that smell, it reminded her of the carefree summer days of her youth. Water splashed over her boots, and she tried to stay on top of the rocks and small grass tufts to keep from sinking in the mud. The endless rain plinked against the surface, driving up the humidity. Unable to take the waterproof material trapping the heat in another second, she wrestled to take her raincoat off. Relief hit her as fast as the rain.

"Good idea. It's like walking through a wet blanket." Ashleigh worked hers off and offered it to her uncle. "Want a turn?"

"No thanks." He took the coat anyway. "I've gotten used to being a drowned rat."

"This feels soooooo goooooooodddddd!" Ashleigh spread her arms and tipped her head back. Her mouth opened to catch the deluge of drops.

Reena seconded the opinion. The humidity suffocated the air.

Finally spying the break in the plants, she tied the coat's sleeves around her waist. It was easier going up this time than down. She used the rungs on the cut-branch ladder to keep her balance until Vincent took over by holding her hand.

The teen had also shed his coat, hanging it off the bottom of a backpack strap. She really should offer to take her pack back, but just the thought of adding the weight seized her cells. She prayed Vincent didn't mind the bur-

den. He'd never tell her if he did, and she had to hope he
didn't feel taken advantage of.

Turning, she spied Nathan eyeing the almost vertical
stairway. "You okay to climb?"

His deep brown eyes flitted to hers, then back to the
branches. "Yeah. My head is pounding in time with the
rain and I've got aches in muscles I didn't know existed,
but I'm sure I can make it up."

Preach, she wanted to say, but remained silent. She
had been feeling like that since her run-in with the tree.

"Want me to stand behind you and push?" Ashleigh
asked. Reena thought she was joking until she saw the
seriousness in the teen's expression.

Nathan clapped her shoulder. "I got it, squirt. Besides,
if I lose my balance, I'd squash you like the bug you are."

"You do wonders for my ego." She flounced up the
branch ladder, winking at Reena when she reached the
cliff edge.

"I'm thinking praying mantis." Vincent limply dangled his hands on his wrists in front of him.

"Gross. They eat their mates." Ashleigh pushed him
out of the way and claimed his spot beside Reena. "I'm
more like a caterpillar about to transition into a butter-
fly." She spread her arms and flapped.

"Uh, no." Vincent positioned himself beside Ashleigh.
"How about a…"

Reena tuned out the Great Bug Debate. She focused
on Nathan…for purely professional reasons. Every wince
that crossed his face and every shudder in his muscles
she felt deeply, er, as in sympathy pains. The pangs in
her heart and soul had nothing to do with his plight. They
were from her own agony. And if she told herself that
enough times, she might believe it.

He exhaled loudly the second he planted both feet on the rocky cliff edge, silencing the teens. "That was fun." His expression screamed the opposite.

"And we're off." Reena started along the edge of the cliff. The stone-laden and dirt trail cutting across the mountain face above had to meet up near the river at some point. Just in case it didn't, she planned to keep an eye on the steep slope. If they had to climb back up the slant, she might pass out for real.

Silver lining? She'd finally get to rest.

Chapter Twenty-Four

Nathan planted the branch he had converted into a walking stick into the leaf-strewn ground and slid his gaze to Reena for the thousandth time in the last hour. Vincent and Ashleigh had scavenged a stick for Reena not long after they'd restarted the trek.

An involuntary tremor rattled the leaves on the small twigs still attached to his stick. He had been attempting to block the terrifying trip down the mountain, but he failed more than succeeded. The utter and complete helplessness was going to haunt his nightmares for a long time. Some adventure junkie would envy him the ride, but Nathan could have lived his entire life without that experience.

Reena lumbered forward, her limp more pronounced and she now favored her left shoulder. As much as she tried to hide it, he didn't miss how heavily she relied on the walking stick. The teens had done an excellent job finding the branch. It was small enough for her height and tiny hands but not so fragile it wouldn't hold her up. And he suspected it was the only thing keeping her from keeling over.

A half hour ago, they had left the wild rocky meadow to plunge back into the forest. *Yay.* Blah. He pulled his stick out of the mud and replanted it with his next step. The landscape was a weird mix of immense trees—he could recognize a few like evergreens, oaks, and maples—sections of vegetation growing only ankle height, and oversized boulders partially buried and/or stacked together. The ground had layers of shed leaves, dead branches, and other detritus. The dank smell of ozone, blooming flora, and decaying bark overwhelmed everything.

Reena had been right about one thing—okay, she'd been right about a lot of things—the thunderstorm had moved out of range. The torrential downpour had become light showers and it gave him hope he wouldn't have to grow gills to survive.

He glanced at Reena, who quickly looked away. Interesting. He had caught her eyeing him more than once, but she always pretended she hadn't been spying. Why? His brain ached something fierce, but this seemed important. *Concentrate.* Before the mudslide, she had been open and teased him. Now? He could practically see a wall around her. As a member of the Aloof Association, he recognized a fellow member. Reena didn't belong in their ranks. She was president of the Sociable Society and aggressively recruited others to join her happy world. Her reversal banged the warning gong.

Reena hobbled on the wide trail. Earlier, they'd walked within inches of each other, now he could drive a truck on the path. He didn't like the space. Well, that wasn't true. He liked not feeling claustrophobic, but this felt like avoidance.

He should be rejoicing, but once again, it felt *wrong.*

He…missed Reena. The epiphany smacked his already throbbing head. As much as he didn't want to admit it, Reena kept him enthralled. The few friends he had were still back in Richmond and, since moving to Bell Edge, he hadn't gotten close to anyone. On purpose. Sure, he had an occasional beer with the guys now working for him, but he wouldn't call them friends. He hadn't noticed the loneliness until Reena. Her brash, adventuresome spirit had barged into his carefully constructed world and made herself at home…then pulled away. This wall she put between them made no sense. The awareness he'd been fighting since they'd set out to find the teens told him her withdrawal had nothing to do with her injuries. They played a major part in her ability to interact, but this went beyond that. She treated him courteously now…like one professional to another. Nothing like the charming, engaging woman who flayed him wide when she got her back up.

That had to change. He wanted to know what transformed her and took her away from him.

Peering over his shoulder, he caught Reena sliding her gaze his way then snapping it forward. Red tinged her cheeks and she lifted her chin. *Curiouser and curiouser.* What a telling reaction…

A dim light of an idea glowed softly. Refocusing his attention, he found Ashleigh and Vincent six feet behind him, strolling as they debated the merits of something. Who knew what the topic was this time. They either seemed to fully agree or vehemently argue a wide range of things. He stopped listening when a discussion about who would win the battle between a vampire and a werewolf got heated. Werewolf, obviously. Ashleigh chose vampire, much to his shame. He'd have to educate his niece. Introduce her to Wolfsbane in the X-Men comics world. A kick-butt female werewolf should change her tune.

Did Ashleigh and Vincent realize their conversations were on par with a first date? The whole feeling the other out, testing reactions, and deciding if they were compatible were the very definition. *He* could see they were compatible. His stomach lurched. He hoped it didn't dawn on *them* for a long, long, looooonnnnnnnng time.

Facing front again, he gripped his walking stick tighter to keep from weaving. His sense of balance had gone bye-bye and the landscape waved like a cruel practical joke. Rubbing his pounding head, he worked to stop seeing three wavy trees on the right. When the trunks lined up, he scraped his tongue across the roof of his mouth. He couldn't get the foul taste and smell of mud to go away. If ever he needed the scent of Reena's strawberries, it was now.

His gaze slid to the youth director. He wanted Reena to talk to him like she used to. To do that, he had to first break down the infernal wall. The easiest way would be to confront her, but visions of her becoming riled and defensive worked against his goal. He shuddered at what would fly out of her mouth. He had to be smarter about his strategy, entice her to shatter the fortress without realizing it. Sneaky? Yes. Did he feel bad about it? Nope. Once he demolished the barrier, he'd find out why she'd put it up in the first place. If he'd done something wrong, he'd apologize.

Let the demolition begin. "Reena," Nathan said with enthusiasm he didn't feel. "Would you rather be the heroine or the sidekick?"

Her walking stick stuttered in the mud and she

snapped her face up to his. Eyebrows drawing down, she tilted her head. "What?"

"In a movie or book," Nathan explained as if it was a normal question, "would you rather be the heroine or the sidekick?"

The crease at the top of her nose deepened. "Are you hallucinating?"

"Now see, me?" Nathan continued as if she hadn't spoken. "I'd want to be the hero." He swished his free hand. "Not for the glory but for the control. I want to call the shots."

Reena snorted. "Of course you would." Her pace resumed.

He lightly elbowed her biceps. "Your turn. Chose."

One second morphed into ten. Just when he thought he'd have to egg her on to answer, the heaviest sigh known to man fell from her lips. "I guess I'd want to be the sidekick."

"Really." He hadn't expected that. "Why?"

She scratched her chin. "While everyone's focusing on the hero or heroine, I can set traps or utilize the time to research ways to stop the villain." Her tone warmed. "No hero or heroine works alone. He or she needs at least one person to support them. They're partners even though one courts more press than the other."

"I never thought of it that way." He was impressed. Her logic made perfect sense and was so *her*.

"Hallelujah. Hallelujah," Ashleigh sang horribly off-key. "The rain has stopped! *Woot!*"

Nathan hadn't even noticed. Stretching his flattened palm, he grinned wide. Only a drop or two falling from the leaves plunked onto his skin, nothing from the clouds overhead.

A squelch blasted behind him and he turned to find Vincent holding the old weather band radio. "...rain clearing," the weatherwoman droned. "The clouds will dissipate in the next hour and clear skies will prevail for the rest of the weekend. Temperatures tomorrow will reach a high of eighty-four and the humidity will be low—" Vincent shut it off.

"Now that's cause for celebration," Nathan exclaimed, raising a fist in the air. He wobbled, lowering it fast, and used his stick to stay standing.

"Yes, it is." Reena brushed her tangled hair back from her face. "Just in time for us to start looking for a place to camp."

"Ashleigh and I can scout ahead," Vincent offered, closing the distance. "I know what to look for."

The word *no* instantly formed on his lips. He didn't want his niece out of his sight.

"We won't go too far ahead," Ashleigh assured, obviously seeing his refusal. She patted Reena's and Nathan's shoulders lightly. "We gotta keep an eye on you, too. Don't want to find one of you facedown. You'd never get up without us."

"Ha, ha, ha, ha," Nathan deadpanned. If it wasn't true, he'd be offended. "Just...be careful, okay? And *pay attention.*"

His niece beamed, then she and Vincent started walking, their pace brisk as they launched into a debate about the best type of campground.

It took Nathan longer than he cared to admit to get reoriented and moving again. His muscles were stiff and his head felt like it had a heavy-metal band wailing in full frenzy. Reena seemed to be battling the same war as him. Weren't they a pair?

"Now," Nathan said, reestablishing his step to walking stick rhythm, "where were we? Ah. Would you rather give up music or television for a month?"

"What is this?" Reena groused, leaning like the Tower of Pisa against her stick.

"It's called fun." He couldn't tell for sure, but he thought, maybe, his plan was working. He'd take grumbling over rigid politeness for sure.

The trill of birds filled the air, calling to each other with song high up in the canopy. So many different chirps, warbles, and whistles made it sound like they were celebrating the end of the rain, too. Birds swooped from the trees. Some chased after each other, and others changed positions to then reignite their song. Squirrels, his least favorite animal now, darted around tree trunks, playing and fighting, while others clamored to the ground to hunt for food.

The forest came alive right before his eyes. "Cool."

"What's cool?" Reena planted her stick and stepped forward. "The Twenty Questions game?"

"Absolutely," he responded. "But I meant the forest coming out of bad weather hibernation."

She swiveled her head, staring up at the canopy. "Yeah. I love it when there's so much life."

He faced forward again. "Okay. Back to my question. Are you giving up television or music for a month?"

"Nathan," she drew out.

"Come on." He gently knocked his stick to hers. "You know you want to tell me." And he looked forward to getting to know her better. He hadn't expected the answers to stupid questions to be insightful, but they were. "I went first last time. Your turn." Was he flirting? Assessing his tone, he realized he was. And it felt good. Wow.

Maybe he did need his head examined. The concussion had changed his thinking a lot. Or maybe it clarified his inner feelings.

Growling, she tapped her stick to his. "Fine. I'd give up television in a heartbeat. I don't watch much anyway. But music? No way. Thankfully you didn't make me choose between books or music, I'd have apoplexy trying to decide."

A bark of laughter flew from his throat. "Good to know your priorities." They passed by a set of boulders stacked on top of each other, their points facing different directions. It reminded him of nature's version of a directional arrow signpost. "As much as it pains me, I'd give up music for a month. It'd be a miserable month and no one would want to be near me, but I'd be worse if I had to live without sports."

She laughed out loud. The pure melody lifted his spirits and had him grinning like a teenager with a crush. *Ohhh*. The epiphanies just kept coming. He *like* liked Reena.

"You are such a typical *guy*."

And that, ladies and gentlemen, was the sound of the wall crashing down.

Chapter Twenty-Five

"There you guys are!"

Ashleigh's exclamation interrupted Reena's laughter. She hadn't realized how much she missed the joy until it filled her. She wasn't sure which was more amazing, that she was still moving or Nathan asking questions that revealed a deeper part of him. If she wasn't hobbling in the middle of the woods on her last legs, she'd swear she'd entered an alternate universe. But no dimension would be cruel enough to have her injured in both realities.

How was she supposed to stay professional when he opened up like this? He had made it clear what he thought about her outlook on life and never seemed interested in connecting emotionally. Then *bam*. One-eighty. Well, maybe not a complete reversal. She bet he still found her positive thinking annoying, but he was genuinely trying to engage her. Teasing…or, if her thumping heart was right, *flirting*. Was he battling an attraction to her? A giddy thrill shot through her veins, reinvigorating her waning energy. Outside of a few teens and her unpredictable, older retirees, she hadn't truly been flirted with in… She couldn't recall the last time. College probably.

Now, a full-grown man who took her breath away showed interest in *her*. It felt incredible. They had fundamental differences for sure, but she sensed in her soul those differences would complement each other like blue and yellow mixing to make green.

"You two are so slow."

Ashleigh's remark jerked Reena out of her spiraling thoughts. Stealing a glance at Nathan, she found him grinning at her. Rats! He'd caught her *again*. Her cheeks couldn't get any hotter. The warmth spread down her neck into her chest. Could she shine a brighter beacon on this attraction? No way he'd missed her ogling.

Ashleigh tromped toward them, smiling wide. "I asked Vincent if he could carry you."

The clouds were thinning overhead, allowing more light to filter through the canopy. It was a shame they were about to lose it for the night. Reena wouldn't mind feeling the sun on her skin. That always strengthened her.

"I thought Reena might go for it," Vincent responded, looking to Nathan, "but I figured you'd crawl before you'd go for a piggyback ride."

Nathan cocked his head. "I don't know," he mused. "If money were involved—"

Ashleigh smacked her uncle's stomach. "You don't extort children," she scolded, her wicked grin belying her words. "You know we're broke. You have to go after the fat cat marks." She shook her head. "Do I have to teach you *every*thing?"

"And on that disturbing note," Reena cut in before Nathan could respond with something just as crazy. "Did you find a spot for the night?"

"Yep!" Ashleigh rocked to her toes. "It's purrrfect." She rolled the *r*'s like a cat.

Reena cut a glance to Vincent. He nodded. "It is." He jabbed a finger at his cohort. "That, without the purr."

"Dud." Ashleigh blew a raspberry at him. "I gave the delivery style."

"Lead the way." Reena motioned, not allowing the teens to launch into another debate.

Ten minutes later, which probably would've been two minutes if she and Nathan were healthy, they stopped in front of the chosen spot. A humongous, abstract rock formation filled the backdrop and low vegetation covered a large swath of land. The trees were spaced wide enough apart that a campfire wouldn't be a danger, and offered plenty of room for tents. If Nathan's was salvageable. If not, she'd figure something out.

"It is purrrfect," Reena repeated, unable to help herself.

Ashleigh cackled and clapped. "Told ya!"

"We even did a little scouting." Vincent fanned his T-shirt, the humidity still thick. "We're not too far from the river. I thought by now the trail would have taken us beyond its reach, but it's past that rock ledge and hill that way." He pointed in the opposite direction from the campsite.

"Ashleigh," Nathan growled, his expression darkening. "You were only supposed to find a camping spot right off the trail." He folded his arms, his walking stick in an elbow crook. "*Not* go off traipsing in the woods."

"But." She toed the earth with her mud-covered blue cross-trainers. "You guys were taking so long, and it's not like the plants are thick like last time."

"We kept an eye on this path for as long as we could." Vincent took a step closer to Ashleigh.

"There are bears in these mountains," Nathan retorted. "And who knows what else."

"They're fine, Nathan." Reena placed a hand on his shoulder; his muscles were like granite. "They shouldn't have gone off without telling us." She shot the teens a reprimanding look. "But, in the spirit of this weekend's focus, they problem-solved on their own. In doing so, they saved us time finding water."

"That does not make it okay." Nathan relaxed and she dropped her hand. It felt a little too homey in that position.

"I agree." Reena glared at the kids. "And they *won't* do something like that again. Right?"

"Promise." Ashleigh bit her lip and peered through her eyelashes at her uncle.

Did he realize how much Ashleigh looked up to him? She hoped so.

"Squirt, you're killing me with those hangdog eyes." Nathan groaned. He opened his arms and Ashleigh *thwumped* against his body. "Don't think they're going to work all the time," he grumbled, kissing the top of her head that just reached his chin.

What a softy. Reena hid her grin behind her fist. He noticed anyway and rolled his eyes.

To keep from fawning any more, she decided to check out the campsite. Limp. Limp. Limp. Limp. Her uneven footsteps and labored breathing filled in the harmony of the birds. The ground was relatively even with leaves and other small detritus covering the mud. The closer she got to the looming rocks, the more she smelled a mishmash of minerals and wet soil along with decay. She inhaled deeply. She loved the scent of nature. The trees gave off a clean odor and the vegetation added to the peace soothing her aches.

Vincent kept pace with her. "We going to attempt a campfire?"

"I want to." Reena studied the area. "If we light it close to the rocks, that'll give the woods another layer of protection."

"There's plenty of small stones to form a protective ring." Vincent pointed toward a grouping near the boulders.

"Excellent. That'll be your job." Reena patted his arm. "Plus, gathering firewood. You remember what to look for when the wood's wet, right?"

"Of course."

Reena tried not to chuckle, but it came out anyway. "Sorry. I guess Nathan's overprotectiveness is rubbing off on me."

Vincent groaned. "Please, no."

Reena's chuckle turned into a full belly laugh at Vincent's horrified expression.

"Cruel," he muttered, then began laughing with her.

"Were you able to fill the water bottle with much rain?"

The smile dropped and he cleared his throat. "Ah, about that."

Reena already knew what was coming.

"Ashleigh and I lost the bottles during the mudslide." His cheeks reddened and he cracked his neck. "I have no clue when. After you yelled 'run,' it all becomes a blur."

Sighing, Reena rubbed the top of her nose. "I'm not surprised. I just hoped that you had put them in the pack to keep your hands free."

"I'm sorry."

She swished her hand. "Not necessary. We'll use what we have tonight and boil some river water before we leave in the morning."

"So, what's the plan, Madam Director?" Nathan asked, coming to a stop on her other side.

"We'll set one tent up on that side." Reena motioned to the left. "The campfire will be in the lee of the boulders, and the other tent will be on the right."

"A girl's side and a boy's side." Nathan nodded. "Just like the summer camps I never attended."

"You got it." Reena straightened as best she could, though she still resembled a leaning octogenarian. "You and Vincent are elected to set up the tents and gather wood. Ashleigh and I are going to wash in the river."

"Hey." Nathan scowled without any heat in his expression. "Why do *we* get the grunt work while you languish in a spa? Is it because we're boys? That's stereotyping, and I protest."

"It's because I was smart enough to call it first." Reena jabbed her stick in the ground like a gavel affirming a verdict. "Ashleigh, would you be so kind to carry my backpack? Be sure to leave the tent behind."

The teen beamed as she pranced to Vincent and took pleasure in unstrapping the yellow-and-gray nylon bag from the bottom of the pack. Water and mud sloshed out of the opening and Reena was extra glad she didn't have to deal with it.

Silver lining: sometimes it was good to be the boss and delegate.

Chapter Twenty-Six

Nathan rested his hands on his hips. "This has to win the award for the ugliest setup." His gaze roamed over the pathetic sight before him. Clucking his tongue, he grimaced at the foul mud taste still coating his mouth. "Do we have anything else we can use for rope?"

Vincent rested one arm on the other and put his chin in his palm. "Not unless you want to use the clothes you're lending me."

"Nah." He hadn't bothered packing much by way of clothing, using the space for a myriad of other things that were going to come in handy now. Thankfully, Ashleigh had talked him into throwing in an extra pair of shorts, a T-shirt, and socks. They were far from new, but they gave Vincent something to wear tomorrow. "We'll just have to hope this holds."

His gaze slid to Reena's tent. They'd had hers put together in less than five minutes. The poles slid in the yellow-and-gray waterproof material with no problems; only the mud coating the inside gave them trouble. It was large enough for two people and had covered mesh vents around the top as well as two zippered doors. His, on the other hand…well, it was erect in a way. The stakes to anchor it were gone and one of the main poles broke when he'd pulled it out of the casing. He and Vincent fed the largest piece of the broken pole into the outside loops and wrangled a thin branch as far as they could into the rest of the loops to form a flat-sided, pointed dome—which should have been rounded. They'd torn his destroyed shirt into pieces and tied the corners of the tent to thick twigs they'd scavenged for stakes, then used his socks knotted together to anchor the top of the tent to the lowest branch of the closest tree, so it didn't collapse. If the thunderstorm had still been raging, it wouldn't have lasted thirty seconds. Fingers crossed, the winds stayed mild tonight.

"I'd take a picture for the award, but…" Vincent waggled his cell phone. The face had cracks throughout and wouldn't power on. Ashleigh's hadn't fared better and Nathan did not look forward to breaking the news.

"I'm sorry." Nathan scrubbed the scruff on his jaw. The mudslide ride or his falling backward into the river had crushed the phone pouch he had shoved in his pack. "You can come with us when we replace Ashleigh's phone. You know she's going to want to get a new one ASAP. I'll replace yours, too—"

"No." Vincent dropped his arm. "Don't—"

"I broke it. I replace it." Nathan put steel in his tone to stop the argument. "Do we have enough wood for the fire?"

The teen's face reddened and he looked like he was bursting to say something about the cost, but he blew out a breath instead. "Yeah. It should be enough."

"Will it burn?" Nathan eyed the wet mishmash stack.

"Sure." Vincent strolled toward the logs. "Once we

prep it." He swiped a jagged stone off a pile and grabbed a dead branch. "You're going to love this."

Thirty minutes later, Nathan still did not love anything about prepping the wood. "You lied to me," he grumped, striking his rock against the log on his thighs.

The deep, rich laugh coming from the serious teen mollified Nathan a tad.

"I'm pretty sure people with concussions shouldn't be acting like cavemen," Nathan continued to gripe. If his headache pounded any harder it might explode his skull.

"Cavemen had it way worse than you do." Vincent showed no sympathy. "Besides, you're not allowed to fall asleep and I need the help."

Another long shaving joined the pile surrounding his boots. "Stop being logical. It's messing with my grumpy."

The kid grinned and grabbed the last log. "You're really cool, Mr. Porter."

"Nathan," he instructed. "Call me Nathan, please, but never Nate." He shot Vincent a look to show he meant it. "We're survivalists." He held up his rock-turned-chisel. "Cavemen aren't formal."

"Ashleigh's lucky to have you." Vincent ducked and concentrated on his piece of wood, trying, but failing, to hide his emotions.

Nathan swallowed around a sudden lump. He remembered what Reena had said about Vincent's father not being around. Nathan couldn't imagine growing up without his own dad. The man was harsh with his lessons at times, but he'd taught Nathan a lot. Memories of fishing trips, baseball games, and backyard grilling filled his mind. For Vincent to miss out on that… Ah, man. Nathan hadn't wanted to let anyone into his fortress of solitude…

now he was inviting two people in. He was getting way more from this trip than he'd expected.

Clearing his throat, he casually shrugged. "I'm not sure how lucky she is, but I'm always around for you, too, if you ever want it." *Argh.* How lame and awkward did that sound?

Vincent's head shot up and he stared at Nathan. Hard.

It took everything Nathan had not to fidget. "I mean it." And it surprised him to realize how much he did. "I'd love a road trip buddy to see the Nationals play the Phillies in DC and in Philadelphia," he blurted, feeling the need to lighten the conversation. "It will pain me to sit next to a Phillies fan, but I can deal with it."

A thin sheen of tears covered the teen's eyes.

"And not just sports," Nathan offered gruffly. "Whatever you need, just let me know. I'll do my best. And that's regardless of your friendship status with my niece."

Vincent cleared his throat twice. "You don't have to pity me."

Nathan snorted. "I definitely do not pity you." His voice roughened again. "I'm impressed, if you want to know, but that's all the confession you're getting out of me." He struck the log. "I'm into being grumpy right now."

Silence prevailed and Nathan let the teen work through whatever emotions swamped him.

"As long as you never call me Vinnie again." Vincent finally spoke. "I might take you up on it."

Nathan briefly wondered how he'd take on Vincent when he was barely surviving Ashleigh. Guess he'd find out. "I reserve the right to use Vinnie when you deserve it."

Vincent's lips twitched. "Right back at you, *Nate*."

Grinning at the teen's cheekiness, Nathan tossed his

peeled wood on the pile, then rested his head into cupped hands. To burn wet branches, they had to chisel off the bark or at least reveal the dry wood beneath. On every piece they gathered. By hand. With rocks. Like cavemen.

Nausea threatened to strike and his headache was epic.

"Is that your tent?"

Ashleigh's exclamation had him twisting on the flat stone he used as a seat. She bounced closer, wearing a clean T-shirt and athletic shorts she must have gotten from Reena. Mud no longer coated her skin and her hair was loose, wet and snarl-free.

"Where's your shirt?" she asked, then cracked up, pointing at the makeshift stakes. "Never mind. That's just sad."

Nathan stood, an unusual shyness gripping him. He had never had a problem going shirtless before, but this felt like the wrong time for that. Something was brewing between him and Reena. The intimacy of getting to know who she was inside excited and unnerved him. Traipsing around with no shirt just felt wrong. Crouching, he snatched his beach towel out of the backpack. Draping it over his shoulders, he crossed his arms to keep it in place. That was the best he could do for now.

"Have a nice bath?" he asked to redirect her focus from his sad abode.

"Awesome." She flung her free arm out, leaving Reena's backpack to dangle on one side. "It feels so good to be clean."

"Took you long enough." Vincent scooped Nathan's pack up. "It's our turn to relish the feeling, too."

The sun had dropped lower. It wasn't set yet, but it was getting closer.

Reena hobbled into view and Nathan's mouth turned to

dust. She, too, had donned a fresh youth group T-shirt and black athletic shorts. Her auburn hair appeared darker when wet and it rested freely just below her shoulders. Scratches and angry bruises dotted her clean, freckled skin… He choked trying to swallow. She was beautiful. Her hazel irises latched on to his and brightened. That small action hit him in the chest. She actually perked up when she looked at him. She didn't roll her eyes or flatten her expression. She *brightened*.

If he wasn't smitten before, he was now. This effervescent woman was even more gorgeous on the inside and she captured his attention completely.

"If you're going to the river," Reena announced, breaking the spell, "you better hurry. The sun setting in the wilderness is different than in town. It gets dark here fast. I didn't mean to take so long, but my hair was a tragic mess."

Nathan couldn't find any moisture in his mouth to respond. Probably a good thing. He'd just stammer something stupid anyway. A breeze brought the most heavenly scent of strawberries to his nose. He inhaled deep, then shamelessly did it again.

Vincent marched in front of Nathan, breaking the spell Reena cast over him. Hopefully, the cool river would restore his senses.

Chapter Twenty-Seven

"You're crazy," Ashleigh exclaimed, jabbing her plastic fork toward Vincent sitting on a log adjacent to her. "Doritos are not the best junk food. Chocolate-chip cookie dough ice cream rules."

"Not just Doritos," Vincent corrected, dropping his spoon into the metal container. "Buffalo-and-ranch-flavored Doritos. Quote me right, Ash. And ice cream? It's good, but sweet does not trump salt."

"I agree," Nathan said at the same time Reena chimed in with, "Sweet and salt are equals."

Every pair of eyes latched on to Reena. She shifted on her log. The campfire snapped and crackled in the center of a ring of stones. The scent of burning wood and beef stew lingered, mellowing her mood. She loved the smell of campfires. So many awesome memories were made sitting on a log watching the yellow and orange flames dance. As she predicted, the forest had grown dark fast. Thankfully, the guys had returned shortly after she could only see dark shapes instead of trees. In minutes, she and Vincent had the fire going, teaching Ashleigh and Nathan the concepts and tricks at the same time. The biggest surprise came when Nathan unveiled small cans of beef stew from his backpack. How he'd lugged those around all day was a miracle, but she was grateful for it. All she had in her pack were zip bags of trail mix and power bars.

Lounging against the boulder formation, she scooped the last of her stew onto her plastic spork. "I mean it," she defended. Nathan sat on a log to her left with Vincent on her right. They all spread enough to form a half moon, facing the trail. "Sweet and salty flavors are equally good, it just depends on your mood at the moment."

"False." Nathan placed his empty can on the ground next to his log. "I've never craved a doughnut, but I get a serious hunger for curly fries."

"I've seen you demolish a box of doughnuts," Ashleigh countered.

Nathan shrugged. "Of course I'm going to eat them if they're in front of me, but I'm not searching them out like I do curly fries. Which, in my opinion, are the best junk food."

"Curly fries are delicious." Reena set her can to the side, her stomach pleasantly full. If only her body would take a break from aching. "But they're not the *best* junk food. That honor goes to tacos."

"Tacos aren't junk food." Nathan sat forward. "That's like saying pizza's junk food." He looked across to Vincent and Ashleigh. "Judges, your verdict?"

"I side with Uncle Nathan," Ashleigh announced. "Dinners aren't junk food. They may not be healthy, but they're not classified as junk food."

"Same," Vincent decreed. "Sorry, Reena. You gotta come up with something else."

"Tough crowd." Reena searched her brain for something else. "Okay. What about cupcakes? I vote for them."

"Kinda broad in scope," Nathan responded, stroking his chin. He had washed the scruff but not shaved it. Secretly, she liked the look. Who was she kidding? She liked the way Nathan looked period. Especially cleaned up and relaxed like he was now. His fresh red T-shirt featured a race car on the front and the title Richmond Raceway. Another pair of khaki cargo shorts, white socks, and his worn boots completed the look. The dark circles and the film of pain covering his eyes made her wince in sympathy. She probably had the same battered appearance.

Tossing a twig at Nathan, she lifted her chin. "Whatever. Cupcakes for the best junk food win."

Ashleigh stood and stretched as tall as she could reach. "I can't keep my eyes open any more. I'm going to bed. Good night."

Vincent gathered her can and placed it with his on a stone ringing the fire. "Great idea. 'Night, all." He walked around the front of the fire and soon disappeared inside the men's wonky tent.

Ashleigh was zipping up their tent when Reena glanced from the tent back to Nathan. She felt awkward and she suddenly didn't know what to do. Should she call it a night? Instant disappointment hit her. She wanted him to *want* to stay and talk to her. She was tired and achy, but her heart longed to find out more about Nathan Porter. Feeling like a schoolgirl with a crush, she hoped he yearned to stay near her as long as he could, too.

The fire snapped and sparks floated in the air. Beautiful, but gave her no clue if she should stand or—

"I've never seen the moon so bright," Nathan mused quietly, his face lifted toward the canopy. "And who knew that many stars existed? I wish the trees weren't in the way."

Tougher than it should have been, Reena tore her gaze

off Nathan and focused on the sky. In the small oval above, a wash of stars winked through the leaves, some brighter than others. The mostly full moon illuminated whatever it touched, lending an ethereal quality to the night. Add in the campfire crackling, an enchanting man, and the forest, and she had an amazing romantic setting. Goose bumps rose the hair on her arms and she shivered at the thrill of it all blending together like a dreamy movie.

"Reena?"

She blinked. Lowering her chin, she found him scooting closer to the edge of his log.

"Hey," he said softly, placing his hand on her forearm. The warmth radiating from his skin to hers brought another round of shivers. "You cold?"

Scalding heat burned her cheeks and she hoped the shadows from the fire hid them. "Not at all." The exact opposite. Nathan had her blood pumping and insides singing. *Speak, Reena*. She had wanted him to stay but all she managed to do was drool and stutter.

His hand left her arm and she instantly missed the connection. He leaned away from her and fiddled with the large pocket on the side of his shorts. "These may not be cupcakes, but hopefully they'll live up to your sweet standards." He pulled out a clear storage bag. A strained chuckle shook his chest. "Ah, they're a bit crushed—"

"Are those homemade chocolate-chip cookies?" Reena breathed, her nose practically against the bag. The scent of the king of cookies made her mouth water and she itched to snatch them.

Nathan's shoulders lowered and his chuckle loosened to pride-filled mirth. "Indeed they are." He waggled the bag.

"Does Ashleigh know you're giving away her hard

work?" Her gaze remained shamelessly glued on the pieces inside.

He yanked the bag against his chest and lifted an eyebrow. "Are you stereotyping?"

"Wha…?" She blinked at the loss of sweet goodness. Then his question sunk in. "Stereotyping?"

"I'll have you know," he replied haughtily, but she could feel the laughter just below the surface. "That *I* can bake."

"You can bake?" she repeated, unprepared for that admission. A hint of shame crept through her at immediately doubting his claim. He just didn't look like a man who knew his way around measuring cups.

"Oh, Ms. Sunshine." He shook his head woefully, still clutching the cookies like a hostage victim. "I don't think I want to share these anymore." He started to put them back into his pocket.

She clamped on to his arm. "No!" The word bounced against the rocks. Clearing her throat, she shifted closer and lowered her voice. "I'm sorry. I did stereotype you. When did you learn to bake?"

He continued to study her with one eyebrow raised. "Hmmmm." He dipped his chin. "You're forgiven." He pulled the bag back out but didn't offer the cookies. "Mom made sure both her sons could cook and bake before we left the house."

Reena's gaze flitted between his face and the bag. "That's awesome."

A sadness crept across his beautiful brown eyes, then they cleared. "At the time, I wasn't so thrilled." He lowered the bag to his thigh. "But when I moved out on my own, I realized the valuable gift she'd shared. And it's really come in handy now that I've got Ashleigh depending on me."

"Did Ashleigh help?" Reena motioned to the cookie pieces, trying to keep her fingers to herself.

Nathan snorted. "If licking the beaters and cleaning up constitutes help, then yes she did." He dropped his head and shook it. "She's hopeless when it comes to actual food prep."

"Ahhhh." A lightbulb went off in Reena's head. "That explains why she always manages to talk someone else into taking her turn for kitchen duties when we host fundraising dinners." She snorted. "I never understood why she always wanted to clean the pots and pans or serve."

He shot a finger gun at her. "Mystery solved."

"Now that I know you've got culinary skills—" Reena pointed at him "—don't think you're going to get out of helping at the next church event."

The sparkle in his expression dimmed and his mouth flattened. "We'll see."

Should she push? She hadn't forgotten their conversation earlier today. He had so much anger at God. She understood the reason, she just wasn't sure if he'd think her intrusive for forcing him to talk about it.

"Speaking of mystery." Reena's gaze fell back onto the bag, feeling God telling her to wait for a better opening. "How about letting me taste one of Nathan's Creations?"

Chapter Twenty-Eight

Nathan held the bag open to Reena, willing his hands to stay steady. His nerves ratcheted to alarming levels and he lost the ability to speak. After he stupidly hyped his baking skills, he worried the cookies would fall short of his bragging. After so many uses, he had his mother's recipe memorized. It would be just his luck if he'd skipped a step this time around.

Reena popped a larger piece into her mouth. The second her lips sealed, she closed her eyes and, with her mouth still full, she groaned. "So good."

He exhaled, glad she didn't witness his relief. "Told ya," he boasted, unable to help himself.

One eye snapped open and zeroed in on him. "I'd normally have an issue with your tone, but you've earned the right to gloat. These are amazing." Her fingers waggled, pantomiming wanting more.

Under the guise of finding the best way to share, he stepped over her splayed feet and plopped onto her log. Only inches separated them and he used that space between them to set the cookie bag. The moment he settled, he feared he'd made a strategic error. The fresh scent of her strawberry soap mingled with the woodsy smell of the fire. Insects singing in the background lent a natural soundtrack to the ultraromantic setting. How was he supposed to concentrate when his senses were overwhelmed with Reena?

She dove into the bag and her knuckles barely brushed his shorts but he felt a jolt of electricity. Goose bumps rose on his skin and he hoped the shadows hid them. Feigning casual, he rested his shoulder blades against a section of the boulder formation. The rough surface helped anchor his mind in reality.

"Can I ask a question?" Reena popped a cookie bit into her mouth.

He reached into the bag to give his hand something to do besides try to hold hers. "Sure."

"Why did you move to Bell Edge?" Reena swiped her fingertips together. "That was stupid. What I really mean is why didn't you move Ashleigh to Richmond?"

He swallowed the cookie. "I wrestled with the decision until I arrived in town." He brushed a few crumbs off his shorts. "It took me less than an hour to see how much she thrived here." He fake shuddered. "No clue why." He winked at Reena's jaw dropping. "Ashleigh had already changed schools once when Scott moved for the new job. I couldn't do that to her again." Memories of that horrible time tried to take hold. He forced them to the back of his mind. "Anyway, I'm a bachelor who owns his own company. Establishing an additional location wasn't hard, so, I sold my house and moved into Scott's, er, I guess my home now."

Reena cocked her head, the firelight dancing over her face.

He wished he could sneak a picture. Everything about

this moment was perfect. If only his cell phone wasn't with Reena's charging on her solar gizmo.

"I've always admired your decision."

He blinked at the admission. Did that mean she'd noticed him before this weekend? Er, beyond being the reluctant new guy at church. He'd have disappeared altogether, but that would hurt Ashleigh, so he'd forced himself to attend every Sunday. At least one of them received comfort during those hours. But now…maybe… he had a new reason to look forward to church.

Reena reached inside the bag and shoved a cookie in her mouth. "I'd mish Ashee sho mwush."

It took him a moment to figure out what she mumbled around the sweet. He was pretty sure it was something like she'd miss Ashleigh so much. "She'd miss you, too," he answered, adding silently, *And so would I.* "But you don't have to worry." He adjusted his position, his spine protesting the stone. "We're here to stay, unless she goes away to college, then I can't vouch for her location or duration."

An owl hooted and he snapped his chin up, hoping to catch sight of the bird. He couldn't find it. The crackle of the fire drew his attention to the flames. Bits and pieces of the day played through his mind and he snagged on one that plagued him. "You were really lucky earlier." He stretched his one leg to the side of the stone ring. The warmth of the fire worked on drying his cruddy boots.

"Hmm?" Reena paused, her hand inches from the bag opening.

The replay of the lightning strike haunted him. "If you hadn't twisted at the last moment, that tree half would have crushed you."

She gazed at her freshly treated palms. No bandages

covered the injuries but she had slathered on a layer of ointment. "It wasn't luck. I heard a voice in my head ordering me to twist. I obeyed without a second thought."

He stilled at the explanation. It sounded eerily familiar.

"I'm sure it was God or one of His angels speaking to me."

God again. She had *no* doubt God helped her. Had He? Nathan had experienced God's benevolence but… His blood began pumping. Nathan had experienced God's *benevolence* in taking Scott but…he'd also survived a mudslide. In fact, he and the rest of the group had survived quite a lot of harrowing things today that should have broken them.

Picking at a newly formed callus on the pad of his palm, he debated sharing. As much as his anger didn't want to admit it, he was sure something similar to Reena's admission had happened to him. "I, uh…" He cleared his throat. "When the mud washed me down the mountain," he tried again. Talking about God out loud or even internally wasn't natural for him. Especially the last six months. Relating his experience felt awkward and clunky, but divine intervention had saved his life. God had saved his life.

He swallowed hard. "I kept hearing a voice in my head telling me how to shift to keep my face above the mud. It even told me to huddle beneath the rock to escape the flow. I would have drowned or suffocated without that voice."

He stared intently at the fire, his body locked tight at the confession.

Reena rested the back of her hand on top of his thigh, near his knee.

He stilled completely.

"Thank you," she said softly. "I can see it was hard and I'm honored you shared your experience with me."

She had no idea. Exhaling and relaxing his muscles, he wanted to entwine his fingers with hers. His hand itched in preparation but he held back, not wanting to mess with the cream healing her palms. The best he could do was drape his fingers over her forearm. The warm connection speared him to his soul.

"When you suddenly disappeared…" Reena's arm trembled. "I've never been so terrified." Haunted hazel eyes wrenched from his to the fire. "I'll never forget the sound of the mud thundering down the mountain."

"Me, neither." He fought the shiver and squeezed her. Then it hit him. Maybe her reason for putting up the wall was her reaction to his almost dying. A slow burn heated him inside. She had been engaging him in conversation and teasing until that happened. If she'd felt the need to pull back that hard, then that could mean she had feelings for him. Colleagues or acquaintances didn't construct needless barriers. Only someone romantically interested and wondering if the other person felt the same would set a boundary. *Ding. Ding. Ding.* His reasoning felt dead-on. A lightness washed over him and he wanted to throw a fist in the air. He wasn't alone in this attraction.

"Why are you smiling?" Reena asked, curiosity replacing her haunted expression. "Has your concussion made you loopy again?"

"Nope." He tried to wipe the grin away but it stuck in place. He couldn't bank on his conclusion. Until he figured out how deep she was invested, he'd keep his feelings to himself. But, man, he hoped he was right. "We've had a day, huh?" he asked to steer her away from pressing harder.

"That makes you happy?" She extracted her arm, much to his disappointment. Fishing another cookie out of the bag, she munched on it.

"Surviving it does." He claimed a cookie piece. "I'm dying to hear a Reena story. Tell me how you got into painting."

She turned and looked him straight in the eyes. "Are you *sure* you're feeling okay?"

"A heavy-metal band has been giving a marathon performance in my brain and my muscles ache," he answered truthfully, shifting forward. He rested his arms around his bent knee and met her stare. "Why?"

Lifting another cookie piece, she tilted her head, wincing at the action. "It's just…" She ate the cookie as if stalling for time. "You're suddenly chatty." She swallowed. "I don't think I've heard you say this much in the entire six months I've known you."

He flinched. He deserved that. "Fair assessment." He plowed his fingers through his hair. How did he explain his interest in knowing everything about her without betraying his emotions? "What can I say, Ms. Sunshine? I'm greedy to know everything about Reena Wells, teen youth director extraordinaire." He inwardly cringed. Had he gone too far?

She kept his gaze for so long, he started mentally scrabbling to fix his blundering.

"I'll trade you," she finally answered. "Story for story."

A huge grin took over his face. "I'm imagining you at two years old, finger painting the walls. How close am I to your creative origin?"

Reena threw her head back and laughed. He cherished the musical sound. "Pretty darn close, actually. It wasn't the walls, it was the newly refinished hardwood floors in the family room."

He leaned his cheek into his hand. "This I have to hear."

One story led into two, then three, and Nathan wouldn't have it any other way. Sleep deprivation had never felt so good.

Chapter Twenty-Nine

Reena clamped a hand over her mouth and yawned so hard, she saw stars. They had only been hiking for an hour but she could barely keep her eyes open. She should have crawled into her tent after she'd shared how she'd started painting, but she hadn't. Nathan had charmed her so completely, she'd ignored her body's plea and stayed up until the early hours trading stories with him. It was the best time she'd ever had. To say she was smitten was an understatement. She was falling in love. No two ways about it. The man she never pictured as hers had captured her heart.

Glorious sunshine emulated the pure happiness pumping through her veins. A light breeze brushed her skin, bringing with it Nathan's wonderful scent. The only dark cloud in her proverbial sky was that she couldn't tell if he felt the same or not. She got the sense he was fascinated with her, but did that translate to real emotions beyond curiosity? He seemed to reach for her a lot. Be it a casual brush or an outright touch, but she couldn't bank on his trying to stay connected as him falling in love, too.

Last night…well, this entire trip, had changed everything for her. She loved her life. Her career wasn't a job, it was a calling she was lucky enough could support her. Offering classes at the community center was so reward-ing, she couldn't imagine not teaching, and her family was the absolute best. But she got lonely. As an answer to her yearning for a partner, God graced her with Na-than Porter.

If she could carry a tune, she'd break into song like the birds surrounding them.

"Did you see that?" Ashleigh asked from her usual position behind her. "A rabbit just shot across the trail and darted into that bush."

The indicated bush shook, then a mostly brown rabbit jumped out the other side and hopped through the trees to disappear behind rocks.

"Today is nothing like yesterday," Nathan commented, adjusting his tilting backpack.

Luckily, Vincent had insisted on carrying Reena's pack again. She didn't argue against it very hard...or at all beyond an "Are you sure?"

"Thankfully," Vincent agreed, walking beside Ashleigh. "I couldn't take another day hiking in that rain or humid-ity."

They wouldn't have had enough water if the air had stayed thick. As it was, she worried the four bottles they'd filled this morning weren't going to last long. "We have to make better time today," she announced, wondering if she could push herself any faster. Her pain yesterday had nothing on today. The level of soreness and stiffness on top of the agony took it to a whole new level. And her palms stung with every minute movement.

"Sure, grandma." Ashleigh imitated Reena's heavy

lean on the walking stick as she shuffled. "We'll be off this mountain in no time."

Embarrassment flooded her cheeks. She looked as ancient as she felt. Great. "Ha. Ha. Ha." Reena faced forward again, her sock-covered hands—her last clean pair—gripping her stick.

"Squirt," Nathan called, his voice stronger and clear today. Hopefully his concussion symptoms had lessened. "Reena's going to bop you upside the head if you keep it up."

"Tempting." Reena rattled her thin branch.

Sunlight brightened ahead like a spotlight and she blinked behind her sunglasses. A small part of her felt guilty for wearing them when no one else had a pair, but her pounding head didn't care about fairness. She had tried to make up for it by offering her bottle of bug spray. She never entered the woods without dousing her skin liberally. Something about her blood enticed the blood-suckers, and she did her best to deny their bite.

"What the…?" Nathan ducked and covered his head.

A second acorn dropped out of the tree, nailing his knuckles.

"Ow." He sprang out of the way and shook his hand. "Did you see that?" Glaring up at the tree, he pointed at a branch. "That squirrel's throwing nuts at me."

Ashleigh and Vincent cracked up.

Reena battled joining them. "I doubt the squirrel aimed for you."

"Wanna bet?" He jabbed toward the gray-brown animal sitting on top of a branch, puffing his tail, and chittering at Nathan. "*Two* nuts hitting me in the head is not a coincidence. He aimed."

Reena lost her fight to stop laughing. The animal

crawled closer to the group on the branch overhead. His tail and chittering picked up vigor. Reena had to admit, Nathan had a compelling argument. "Why do squirrels have it in for you?"

"I have no idea." He threw his hands up. "They declared war for no reason."

Tears streamed from Ashleigh's eyes. "Uncle Nathan, I wish I could take a video. This is priceless."

A twig suspiciously rocketed toward Nathan.

"That's it." He pivoted and began marching, his walking stick slamming into the ground with every step. "If I was a hunter," he called over his shoulder, "we'd be having squirrel for lunch. You hear that, Squirrel! You'd be lunch!"

Reena clung to her branch, laughing so hard, her vision blurred.

"Do squirrels have a gossip network?" Vincent asked, wiping his eyes with the heels of his palms.

"Apparently." Ashleigh straightened from leaning on Vincent. "This can't be the same squirrel from the downed tree. He'd stay pretty close to his nest, right?"

"Unless his nest was destroyed when the tree fell over," Vincent mused.

Reena peered up at the furry troublemaker. It couldn't be the same one, could it? What were the odds it followed them? No. Tracking squirrels? That was crazy-toons. Jamming her stick into the ground, she rallied. "Let's go, troops. Nathan's getting away from us—"

"And who knows what might happen to him next," Ashleigh finished, jogging past Reena to catch up to her uncle.

Vincent strolled beside Reena. "He does seem to be a magnet for calamities, huh?"

Reena nodded. "I don't think he'll volunteer to chaperone the next camping trip." A pang pierced her heart. She loved nature and couldn't imagine living without the majestic beauty. Especially in a mountain-based town. Exploring the forests and hiking the trails pumped in her blood and she hated the thought of not sharing it with Nathan.

Vincent snorted. "I'd be shocked if he did." He shrugged. "But he could surprise us. I can't imagine him letting Ashleigh camp without him."

That bothered Reena. If Nathan enjoyed communing with nature, then she could appreciate his joining in, but if he tagged along because he didn't trust his niece and, by extension, Reena, then she had a serious issue.

The tree line ended at a vast clearing. "Hold up," Reena whispered, clasping Vincent's tanned forearm. She plucked her cell phone out of the backpack's side zipper pocket. Her sock-covered hands made taking a picture near impossible. It took too many tries before the sensor recognized enough heat to snap one shot then a second for good measure.

The Porters stood at the apex of an old stone bridge. Ashleigh had her hand wrapped around Nathan's biceps, animatedly pointing at something in the peaceful water below. Nathan grinned, staring down at his niece. Sun caressed their matching brown hair, highlighting her lighter streaks and his thicker scruff. The image was idyllic and worthy of a painting. The idea of committing it to canvas jazzed her as much as the mental photograph she envisioned of Nathan so clearly yesterday. Looked like she'd found a new muse.

"Thanks for waiting, Vincent." She checked the calling signal. Still nothing. No data indicator, either. Zipping the phone away, she patted his shoulder. "Go ahead."

The teen jogged to the two on the bridge.

A lazy river, so still it was almost a lake, flowed beneath a beautiful tan-and-gray stone bridge. The sides ended at Nathan's and Vincent's waists and sported a smooth, flat stone topper, wide enough to sit on, which Vincent and Ashleigh clamored to do now. Nathan handed water bottles and power bars to the teens, then opened a bar for himself. The arch below the apex had a symmetrical design of long, flat stones like bricks curving from one side to the other.

Reena ambled out of the trees and onto the pebbled path, inhaling the variety of flowering bushes growing rampant along the water line. The sun soaked into her skin, rejuvenating her waning energy.

"Turtles!" Ashleigh pointed to the water. "Look!"

Nathan smiled at Reena, a twinkle lighting up his pretty dark brown eyes.

Warmth instantly flooded her cheeks that had nothing to do with the sun or temperature. Nor could she stop her returning smile if her life depended on it.

He motioned for her to join him and her blood juiced at his invitation. As if they had a mind of their own, her feet headed straight for him before she realized she was moving. Yep. Definitely falling for this man.

"There's a whole flock?" His mouth twisted. "Group? What do you call a bunch of turtles?"

"A bale." Why she knew that, she didn't want to reveal. Documentary television had kept her company for too many years. She leaned against the bridge's side and peered over. Four small dark heads poked just above the surface, their feet lazily swimming beneath. Two heads darted underneath the water, their shelled bodies heading toward the bottom to blend in with the rocks.

Heat encompassed her left side and goose bumps rose on her arms. Nathan stood within inches, his right hand so close to her socked left one resting on the ledge, she wondered if he would close the distance. "It's really pretty here," he murmured softly, not that the teens could hear beyond their conversation about turtles. Each tried to out-knowledge the other. Finally, a worthwhile argument.

Reena nodded. "Told ya the mountain was beautiful." She inhaled again, this time nature mingled with Nathan's musk. If she bottled the scent, she'd make millions.

"Here." Vincent nudged her shoulder with the edge of a water bottle, his feet swinging as they dangled. "I saved the rest for you."

She gratefully took the offering and finished the other half. The plastic crinkled and dented, startling the ambient turtles.

"Aw." Ashleigh pouted. "They're gone."

Nathan unwrapped a sports bar and the scent of peanuts and raisins assaulted her. "Gourmet food at its finest." He thrust the bar toward her. "Eat up."

"You're talking to a woman who thinks tacos are an awesome food choice." Reena snatched the bar from him, her stomach growling. The baggie of trail mix for breakfast had already worn off. "I don't do much gourmet eating."

"My kind of woman." His cheeks flared and he yanked his gaze away to stare hard at the water. His grip on the ledge tightened and he leaned back as far as his arms would allow, then forward again. In the rocking, she caught him sneaking a peek at her out of the corner of his eye.

A chorus of clapping erupted in her brain. Taking a bite, she almost couldn't chew with the huge smile plastered on her mouth. She'd found her silver lining for the morning: Nathan Porter liked her beyond a curiosity. He might even *like* like her.

She fell a little deeper in love.

Chapter Thirty

Nathan couldn't believe the difference the sun made. Yesterday, the forest had been a dark, creepy place, perfect for horror movies. Today, it felt full of life, adventure, and beauty. Minus the vindictive squirrel declaring war, the day was turning out perfect.

The path they trekked this morning was narrower than yesterday afternoon's section, but not as tight as the part with the downed tree. Vegetation covered the forest floor on both sides, resembling the wild mass he and Reena had first encountered when they'd searched for the teens.

For the billionth time, his gaze slid to the enchanting woman he *constantly* thought about now. A giddiness tingled his veins at finding her eyes already on him. *Score.* He wasn't the only one sneaking peeks and grinning like a fool at getting caught. Her skin looked beautiful with a blush; his, not so much. He wished he had packed a battery-powered shaver. His scruff itched to the point of distraction and was turning into a scraggly beard. Not attractive. He wanted to keep Reena's attention, not repel her by becoming a grizzly man.

Sunlight winked through the canopy of leaves overhead, throwing abstract shadows, and dancing spots everywhere. Maybe he should've put on the sunblock Reena offered before they'd broken down the campsite. Too late now. They had already taken a break on the quaint bridge a half hour ago and they had a decent momentum going. His sympathy rose for Reena's limping and wincing. His concussion headache had thankfully dulled and his thinking was clearer, but it looked like she struggled more today.

"Ms. Sunshine," he said softly, the peace of the forest inspiring him to almost whisper. It was probably stupid. The birds carrying on with their lives were loud enough to drown everything out. "If you won ten thousand dollars, what would you do with it?"

"Do you have an endless supply of these off-the-wall questions?" Reena shook her head, an eyebrow rising.

"A *deer*!" Ashleigh squealed.

The long-legged, brown doe—at least he thought it was a doe since it had no antlers—on their left snapped her head up. Black eyes studied them, her big ears twitching forward, then she bolted in the opposite direction.

"Subtle, Ash," Vincent deadpanned.

"Oh, shut up." Ashleigh pushed Vincent, but he only swayed.

"Where do these questions come from?" Reena pressed, pulling Nathan back into their conversation.

"Uhhhh." He cleared his throat. Did he confess or make something up? "My last girlfriend was obsessed with dating sites."

Reena's head whipped toward him so fast he worried she'd added whiplash to her list of injuries. "What? I have so many questions."

"Yeeaaahhhh." He scrubbed his hair with his free

hand. He should have made something up. "Um. She had profiles on I don't know how many sites, but she didn't go on dates while we were together."

"I don't get it." Reena's stick jammed into the drying ground, helping her up the steepening incline. "Why bother if she didn't use them?"

Argh. He shouldn't have said anything. "She did use them," he confessed, then rushed to explain. "We didn't have a steady relationship. We were broken up as much as we dated." He eyed a squirrel running across a boulder next to him. "When we were on again, she'd quiz me, using the lists the sites provided to facilitate first dates." The squirrel jumped and landed on a tree branch, heading away from him. "I, uh, remember the fun ones, I guess."

"Sooooo." Reena tightened her ponytail. "I shouldn't think twice about the fact you're asking me the same questions your ex-girlfriend asked you?" She hobble-stuttered to a stop. "Wait." Her face turned toward his but he couldn't see her eyes behind the dark sunglasses. "She *is* your ex, right?"

Nathan loved the sharpness in her tone. It was another confirmation his theory about her interest in him was correct. Taking advantage of the pause, he lowered her shades to the end of her cute nose. "One hundred percent my ex." He held her gaze. "A relationship *never* to be resurrected again." He hid a shudder at just the thought of reuniting with Tracy. The woman was the epitome of high maintenance and spoiled. Tracy was everything the opposite of Reena. Wow. He hadn't realized that. And yet, Reena was the opposite of everything he'd thought he wanted. It messed with his head. How could he be falling for this perky antithesis of what he sought in a partner? It didn't make sense. Yet his soul had never talked to him before Reena.

She shoved the glasses back in place and resumed walking.

Silence descended and Nathan cracked his neck. He should've made something up. Talking about his ex had obviously been the wrong move—

"I'm glad you're not with her anymore," Reena stated quietly, knocking her stick against the side of his boot gently. "You deserve so much better." Her white sock rubbed across her freckled nose. The adorable brown spots kept appearing across the bridge the longer the sun caressed her face. "I can't imagine seeing someone who actively kept profiles on dating sites. It's like she's telling you without saying anything that you're not a priority and easily replaceable."

She had summed up his feelings for Tracy exactly. "And now you get why I will *never* date her or anyone like her again." He snorted. "I shouldn't have taken Tracy back after the first time we broke up." He rubbed the sides of his mouth. "I don't have a good excuse and I'm embarrassed to admit it was easier to pick up where we left off than to start all over again with someone new."

"You're right." Reena elbowed his arm. "You should be embarrassed with that heartwarming reason."

"Like you've never regretted a relationship before," he retorted, cocking an eyebrow.

A flush worked its way from her hairline to disappear into her T-shirt. "I, uh, haven't." Her stick jabbed into the soft earth, leaving a divot in its wake. Her eyes slid to his, then back to the path. "I can't say I've dated much."

He slammed on the brakes and gaped. "No way. You're messing with me."

His favorite laugh crossed her chapped lips. "You're good for my ego, Nathan Porter."

"Ooooooh," Ashleigh crooned, drawing to a stop beside him. "Is there something juicy going on up here? What are we talking about?"

"Your uncle," Reena said at the same time Nathan stated, "Ms. Sunshine is trying to get one over on me."

Vincent's gaze swung between Reena and Nathan. The teen studied them closer, then blinked repeatedly. His jaw fell open and he rocked back on his heels.

Nathan shook his head the tiniest bit, signaling to the guy not to say a word. He no longer had to wonder if his attraction to Reena was as obvious as that white flower on the shrub. Awesome. He loved having his burgeoning emotions on display for one and all to read. Especially when he hadn't figured them out for himself yet.

"I have a bigger question," Vincent intoned, pointing ahead of the group. "Reena, is that the crossroads you were talking about yesterday?"

Nathan wanted to hug the teen right then and there. When floundering, distract, distract, distract.

Reena pivoted on her heel, using her stick for balance. "If so, we made better time than I realized." She hobbled forward. Standing in the center, she peered at the path that continued relatively straight ahead, then at the one forking to the right. "Yep. This is where we make a decision."

Nathan waltzed to the intersection and scanned both trails. He didn't see much difference between the two. The one forking to the right had a steeper incline, but they had been tackling uneven terrain since they'd started this journey. It didn't really mean anything. At least, he didn't think it meant anything now.

Flattening his hand across his eyebrows, Nathan shaded his eyes from the midday sun. "Can you remind me again what the differences are between the two?"

Ashleigh perched on the edge of a stone half buried in the ground in the shade. Fern branches enveloped her arms and she kept swatting them away.

Vincent positioned himself at a perfect point to create a triangle that didn't favor one side over another. Looked like Nathan had won the teen over. Every other time, Vincent always stood closer to Reena.

A white-socked hand swiped at an errant hank of hair escaping Reena's ponytail. "This path—" she motioned to the right fork "—leads to a ranger station. It's a shorter distance overall, but we'll have to traverse an extremely steep climb, think almost wall face, to reach the rest of the trail."

Nathan's stomach clenched. He did not like the sound of that. "And that one?"

Reena jabbed toward the other path with her stick. "That one leads to a highway. We should be able to pick up a cell signal once we reach the road or flag someone down."

"But…" he encouraged, knowing something about rocks was coming.

"The path winds through the mountains," she answered in a tour guide tone. "It's a longer hike and it has a large boulder outcropping we'll have to scale."

Nathan drove a hand through his hair and pulled. Tromping away, he glared at the myriad of trees growing on every side of the trail. "Those are our only choices?"

"Yes." Reena leaned on her stick, facing him.

His boots kicked up dead leaves as he continued pacing from one side to the other, his walking stick jabbing into the ground. "Treacherous steep climb or scaling boulders." He paused. "Isn't there a third option?" One that didn't endanger his niece's or Reena's life?

"Not anymore," Reena answered. "The wooden bridge to the benign side surfed down the river."

Nathan lifted his gaze to the canopy. Yesterday's mudslide had driven home how quickly Ashleigh could become a total orphan. His heart constricted just as his brain coughed up Ashleigh's description of the river current trying to drown her. He could easily lose her, too.

"Personally," Reena continued, "I think we should head for the ranger station."

"That's the one where we climb a wall, right?" Nathan pivoted to pace in the other direction.

"Yes." Reena nodded. "But it's a shorter distance to call for help."

"I agree with Reena," Ashleigh announced, fanning herself with the fern. "It makes sense, and I want to go home sooner than later."

Nathan headed toward his niece. "I love you, squirt." He stroked her loose hair tangling from the breeze and nature. "But you're not the best at thinking through all the consequences of a decision. Your impulsive nature gets you in trouble. A lot."

Her smile vanished. Nathan hated that, but he had to be honest. Filling her with false platitudes and empty praise only hurt her in the end. This was one lesson he was going to drum into her head if it killed him: think *before* she leaped.

"How many times do I have to say I'm sorry?" she retaliated, yanking her head from his hand.

"Mr. Porter," Reena stated with too much precision.

"Are you saying *I'm* not the best at thinking through all the consequences, either?"

At Reena's challenge, Nathan sighed. He scrubbed his face and moved to within two feet of the director. "I'm saying this weekend didn't go as planned."

Red encompassed her cheeks at the same time her skin whitened around the corners of her compressed lips.

Man, how had he ended up in this position? He wasn't trying to be a jerk. But he wasn't going to rewrite or avoid history, either. "Decisions and assumptions were made that ultimately led us here."

"You mean decisions *I* made." Reena shoved her sunglasses to the top of her head, her eyes sparking with fire. "Don't dance around an issue. If you have something to say, then say it plain."

"I don't want to fight with you, Reena." Nathan lifted his arm but stopped shy of connecting with her hand wrapped tightly around her walking stick. "I'm just stating simple facts."

"Facts." Her lip curled. "Yeah." She snorted. "The buck does stop with the director, doesn't it? All the blame falls on me."

"Reena." Nathan wanted to howl at the ice dripping off her biting words. "I'm not attacking you personally—"

"Of course you are," she shot back. "*My* decisions *are* personal."

"*My* main concern is Ashleigh." He jabbed a thumb over his shoulder, trying to get Reena to understand who was at the heart of every choice he made now. Though, if he was honest with himself, he *didn't* fully trust Reena's decisions. Her adventurous spirit and everything's-positive outlook didn't factor in the ramifications of taking on more than they could handle. Hence, them trapped on a mountain and standing in the middle of an intersection arguing about it. To be fair, his niece owned a portion of their circumstances, too.

"Hey," Ashleigh snapped. "I'm fifteen years old. I'm not a baby you have to coddle, Uncle Nathan."

"You're right." Nathan turned just enough to include his niece in the conversation. "You *are* too old to coddle, but that doesn't mean it isn't my job to protect you. Climbing up a near vertical wall is insane. Neither of us has that kind of experience. It's dangerous to even try."

"But we're not boulder climbers, either." His niece pushed off the stone and positioned herself next to Reena.

Point made. She sided with the youth director. Got it. "It's still the safer of the two options."

Vincent maintained his neutrality, like Switzerland.

"It'll take a lot longer to reach the highway." Reena met Nathan's gaze, the sparks still flashing in her eyes.

"True," he agreed, locating his stomach near his knee. He had lost all the ground, and possibly respect, with Reena. His soul bleated and he wanted to hurl his stick in sorrow. Despite his epiphany that he was falling for the animated woman, it came down to a bitter choice. Put all his trust in Reena's recommendation or follow his gut on the best way to protect Ashleigh.

He couldn't take any risks with his niece. "I stand by my decision. We should take the path to the highway." He brushed Reena's socked hand. "You are in no condition to climb a wall." Ignoring the stiffening beneath his touch, he maintained the connection. "You're one of the strongest people I know, but your body has reached its limit. As mad as you are at me, you have to admit it. You're not up for that challenge."

Chapter Thirty-One

Reena slammed her walking stick into the soft ground. A divot of drying mud plopped to the side when she lifted it. Liking that, she slammed her stick into the ground again with her next step. Putting holes in the trail was a lot better than adding one to Nathan Porter's forehead.

For the last…who knew how long—two hours? three?—she'd stewed on his words. With a bloodthirstiness she hadn't experienced before, she silently plotted all the ways she could use her stick on him. How dare he imply she didn't think through consequences of a decision? More mud flung to the side. Then have the gall to say he wasn't attacking her personally? Right. As if her decisions could be anything other than personal in the woods.

Slam. Divot. The insinuation she wasn't concerned for Ashleigh's safety had her strangling the branch. Of course, she was concerned. She wanted *all* of them to be safe.

She half turned to glare at him but forced herself to face forward. The teens had surpassed her a while ago, and Nathan had appointed himself into some overwatch position. He traipsed behind her, not hovering but ready to jump into "rescue mode" if she stumbled. That only made her madder. She wasn't a vulnerable damsel in distress. Yes, she was aching from head to toe and needed medical attention, but still. She'd rather fall on her face than have him swoop in.

Okay. Falling on her face might be going a bit too far, but being seen as a simpering female got to her. Her heart argued that he'd admitted she was the strongest person he knew. That his statement didn't sound like a man who thought her weak or a damsel in distress. He sounded like a man who'd watched her struggle for two days and called her on it *plainly*, like she told him to.

Growling under her breath, she smacked her stick into the ground again, satisfied at the plop of mud flinging to the side.

She hadn't brought them to the impossible choice—circumstances had. Without the bridge, Reena didn't know any other way to get help but these two paths she remembered from her research. And that thought drove to the heart of her fury. He didn't trust her. Not when it came to big decisions anyway. He trusted she could set up a camp or start a fire and other small things, but anything involving heightened risk, he discounted or flat-out distrusted her.

Two more divots pitched sideways. She had thought they had gotten past his initial distrust with all the conversations and companionship they'd shared, especially last night, but obviously not. Her soul slowly withered, the radiance of their newfound closeness bleeding away. How could she even consider a relationship with little to no trust on his part? She couldn't…*wouldn't*, no matter how much her heart wanted the man.

The pain slicing through her heart compressed her chest like an anvil.

Her palms screamed at her to ease her grip and her body cried for her to stop killing the ground.

Slowing her pace from a limping march, she loosened her hold. The trail had meandered through the mountain like a lazy river. The forest gave way to clearings filled with undergrowth and flowers, then would accede some ground to large rocks and rushing rapids in streams. She barely noticed any of it. Kicking the end of her stick, she wanted to growl again. Nature's sun-dappled magnificence was her favorite part of hiking.

Maybe Nathan had made a few solid arguments—

"Oh, wow," Ashleigh exclaimed, jerking Reena back into her surroundings.

"Oh, wow," Reena echoed.

Massive natural stone monoliths rose out of the ground to form a triangular rock tunnel. Inside, wide bands of minerals waved in patterns and deep crevices etched in the stone she could use to climb, not that there was anywhere to go. Looking left and right, she could find no way around the formation. The trail continued through with leaves and dirt covering a stone pathway.

"This is so cool." Ashleigh roved her hands, her fingers scraping against the rough surface.

"Literally." Vincent also fingered the stones.

Goose bumps rose on Reena's arms and she fought a shiver. The temperature had dropped at least ten degrees in the shade and rocks. Without the sun, the tunnel had a dark, imposing feel. The trail through curved just enough that she couldn't see the other side, adding to the mystique.

A wall of heat scorched the back of her left arm, but

she ignored Nathan. He made it tough by standing only inches behind her and enticing her with his alluring scent, but she remained strong.

"Whoa," he breathed, brushing his arm against hers. "Is this natural?"

The connection hit her deep in her soul, pausing the withering for a moment. A moment too long in her book. The man didn't trust her.

"I think so," she answered as flat as possible. Without a handy map or internet signal, she could only guess, but something about the formation didn't seem man-made. Digging her walking stick in the ground, she stepped through the entrance.

Ten feet overhead, sections of the monoliths met. Neither had smooth surfaces. Large bumps and valleys with crevices and striations ran throughout. The trail was only wide enough for one person, so they formed a line. As she trekked deeper, spots of sunlight broke through spaces where the rocks didn't fall flush. *Interesting.* Carefully sliding the sock off her left hand, she touched a second abutting rock. The stone iced her fingertips and the heavy smell of minerals filled her nose. This tunnel wasn't made up of one large rock like they had encountered with the downed tree, but huge boulders snugged together.

She twisted sideways to fit through a narrow crevice made by two bulging sections and got her first glimpse of the other end of the trail. Moisture dried in her mouth. The formation acted like a chute, funneling them into… the sky. *Rats.* She had hoped they would find a way to circumvent tackling the boulders. But no. They had come upon the part of the trail she had been dreading.

Reaching the end, she paused by the left side of the triangular exit and leaned her hand against the rock. The rough surface bit into the scrapes on her palm, stinging her injuries. Puffy white clouds in a powder-blue sky and the sun shining bright greeted her when she stared straight ahead. Tops of trees and a valley continued in her line of vision as she brought it down to finally land on a pile of boulders with no rhyme or reason to the mound, starting at her feet. The tan, gray, and dirt-covered stack was haphazardly compiled with gaps, sharp edges, flat sections, and drop-offs.

Ashleigh and Vincent squished beside her to fill the exit completely.

"We're climbing down those?" Vincent asked, shifting his feet and scrunching her and Ashleigh in the process. "You said boulders, but I didn't picture them looking like this."

"Like what?" Nathan asked, all but pressed against her and Ashleigh's backs, their heads only reaching his chin.

Reena inched forward as best she could without letting the teens know she was escaping Nathan's touch.

Whether Nathan noticed or not, she didn't know because he jolted at the same time and scoffed, "These are the boulders? You're kidding, right?"

She didn't bother answering. She hadn't known what to expect only having seen a marking on a map, but… wow.

Nathan scratched the back of his neck, his mouth thinning, and his jaw muscle pulsating.

Reena tried to not watch him out of the corner of her eye, but her traitorous gaze sought him out despite her stern stance that Nathan was no longer a possibility.

Vincent carefully walked to the end of the jutting rock leading out of the tunnel. Crouching, he rested his palms on the sunny surface and peered over. Before she could stop him, he twisted his lower half and jumped, landing on another boulder. With only his head and neck visible, he peered back at the group. "It's doable."

Reena clamped a hand on her pounding heart. "I am going to wring your neck, Vincent Clark. You scared me to death!"

The teen grinned, not fazed at her threat one bit. He knew she'd never hurt him, but still. He should at least pretend to be cowed. *Grrrrrrrrrrr.* Teenagers and their terrifying invincibility blinders. The "nothing bad would ever happen to *them*" mentality was going to make her go gray early.

"Come on, Ash." Vincent waved. "I'll help you down."

Nathan stiffened. "Ash—"

"I'll be careful." Ashleigh peered over her shoulder, then back to Vincent. "I don't need your help, *Clarky.*" She strode forward, her balance perfectly centered. "Move it." She made shooing motions.

Vincent's head disappeared just as another thump reached Reena's ears.

She winced. Her body was going to revolt after the first jump down. Resting her walking stick against the rock wall, she gave it one last pet to say goodbye, then moved to the boulder's end.

Ashleigh had made it to the lower boulder, while Vincent had two arms out and walked with one foot precisely in front of the other to traverse a narrow rock ledge.

Should she keep the socks on her hands or take them off? The socks could make her grip slippery, but the harsh surfaces would chew her already injured palms to pieces. *Sockless for better traction*, she decided, shoving the white cotton into the side pocket on her fitness shorts.

"You want to go first or me?" Nathan asked, speaking directly to her for the first time since the argument.

Her muscles stiffened and she purposefully kept scanning the rock formation. She hoped he didn't see the pain in her soul that had nothing to do with her injuries. "I'll go," she answered to end any chance of a conversation.

She copied Vincent's twist and landed on the lower boulder. *Owwwww!* She wasn't as tall as the teen, so her jump was farther and her landing harder, rattling every bone and muscle in her body. Using the rocks, she held on as best she could and limped to the next edge. Tears crowded the corners of her eyes at the wounds reopening on her palms and her hips throbbing with agony.

Ashleigh reached the tightrope walk on the narrow ledge and seemed to have no issues.

Reena studied the rocks in front of her and found that if she stretched, she could put one foot on that rock there then kinda hop with the other foot to make it to another flat section. Blinking at the moisture blurring her vision, she went for it. Wobbling her landing, she slapped her palms against the closest rock. Her bloody handprint marked the rock and she couldn't stop the tears falling silently down her cheek.

Nathan thumped to the boulder she had just vacated and crouched. "Reena—"

"No!" Vincent yelled. *"Ashleigh!"*

A chilling scream raised every hair on Reena's body.

Chapter Thirty-Two

A high-pitched, terrified scream pierced Nathan's ears. One second his niece was standing at the edge of a boulder. The next second, she disappeared.

"Ashleigh!" Vincent yelled at the same time as Nathan.

A horrifying *thwump* echoed and Vincent's deep cry pierced the air. Another round of high-pitched screaming began, this time in agony.

The blood froze in Nathan's veins and he panicked. "Dear God, help me," he kept repeating like a mantra, searching wildly for a way to get to Ashleigh.

"This way." Reena motioned him to hop-jump to her boulder.

The screams turned into tortuous wailing, driving Nathan mad.

You can't have her, too, God. He jumped and landed, a boot sliding off the rounded edge. Reena clamped a hand around his forearm and tugged. He slapped his palms against the flat boulder in front of him, blinking at a bloody handprint. Unable to understand its meaning, he scanned for a way down. He had to get to Ashleigh. She needed him. *Now.*

Ash-leigh. Ash-leigh, his heart pumped, clouding his thinking. He couldn't let her down. *Ash-leigh. Ash-leigh.*

"Nathan."

His gaze pitched and skittered, then landed on Reena. Small lines of blood smeared her face and he couldn't comprehend why. She squeezed his forearm *hard*.

The agonized wails were now coupled with sobbing so wrenching he couldn't stop his own tears from falling. "Ashleigh," he choked.

"Vincent," Reena yelled. "What's happening?"

"She's hurt…bad," the teen wheezed, barely audible. "I think…she broke…a leg."

God, no. Nathan blacked out for a second. *I have to reach her. I'll never utter an angry word about You taking Scott again if you get me down there.*

"Pay attention," Reena barked. "Pull yourself up." She pointed to the top of a narrow ledge a little over his height.

He didn't think twice. He gripped the rough stone and muscled himself up, then managed to get his feet planted on the thin strip. Widening his stance, he crouched, and offered a hand to Reena. She clamped on and a warm moisture coated his palm, making his grip slippery. She jumped at the same time he lifted. For one terrifying moment, he thought he was going to lose his balance and fall off, but she must have sensed trouble. She used her boots on the rock to help them both. With all his strength, he stood up. It worked. She wobbled beside him on the ledge and he stared at his skin.

Blood? "What—"

"Don't worry about it." Reena turned her back on him. "Keep going."

"Uncle Nathan!"

Nathan lost all semblance of rationality. "I'm coming, Ashleigh." His feet began moving before his brain engaged. Ignoring caution on the narrow ledge, he ran until he reached Reena blocking him from getting to his niece. *Move. Move. Move.*

Reena slapped her palms against the edge of a tan-colored, concave boulder and hopped, planting her right boot on top. Gory handprints smeared in the dirt as she straightened. Yelps of pain mixed with tears falling onto the dirt and blood.

He waited a scant second for her to clear, then hopped on top of the boulder. Using his arms for balance, he surpassed Reena, jogging the uneven surface that angled fifteen degrees higher in the front than the back. He reached the edge and peered down. All the oxygen left his head. He dropped to his knees, the stone biting into his skin, but he didn't care. Ashleigh lay on her back, sprawled on top of Vincent. Her right leg was bent in an unnatural position and she screamed as she cried.

"Ashleigh," Nathan croaked, digging his fingertips into the boulder until they screamed with his niece.

"Uncle...Nathan," she puffed, her skin so white, she looked ghostly.

"She's in shock," Reena announced as if reading his mind, kneeling beside him.

"I have to get down there." He frantically searched for a way to reach his niece. He twisted to lower himself over the edge. Reena grabbed the back of his shirt and stopped him. "Let go," he barked, pulling to break free.

"Not that way." She tugged against him. "You'll land on them."

He met her gaze, allowing the terror and panic to shine without a filter. "I *have* to get down there."

"Follow me." She stood and limp-jogged to the back of the boulder.

He only paused a moment to consider jumping anyway, but couldn't risk hurting his niece. In seconds, he reached Reena's side and she motioned to the left.

"If you're careful," she stated, using a pointing finger as she talked, "you can pick a path alongside this boulder. See—"

He instantly saw what she meant and didn't need any more instruction. Scrabbling, climbing, teetering, and clawing, he finally reached the flat section of boulder with the teens.

Crawling to his niece's side, he brushed the hair off her face. "I'm here, squirt. I've got you."

Her screams reduced from ear-shattering to hard crying and whimpering.

"Can't…bree…eathe," a deep voice wheezed. A sickly attempt at an inhale followed. "He…lp."

"Vincent." Nathan's brain cleared enough to understand the logistics of what must have happened. The teen had probably tried to catch Ashleigh but couldn't counteract her momentum. She'd landed on top of him, breaking her leg and probably cracking one or more of his ribs.

Fresh tea. "God, what do I do?" he hoarsely cried, assessing the teens. Should he move Ashleigh or move Vincent? Vincent's ribs could puncture his lungs if they hadn't already, and Ashleigh's bones and ligaments could rupture or tear more. This was an impossible decision.

"Nathan."

He snapped his head up at Reena's thready voice.

She swayed beside him, dripping blood and tears. Somewhere along the way, she had lost her sunglasses.

"Can you lift Ashleigh's upper body? I can help slide Vincent from underneath."

"You can barely stand, let alone pull a growing man," he countered, anguish fuzzing his mind. He couldn't take Ashleigh's pain away and it was killing him.

She weaved to the other side of the teens and cracked her knees against the boulder. She cried out but continued on with her purpose. "Vincent, this is going to hurt like mad, but you're going to have to help me. Okay?"

The teen nodded, his skin as pasty as Ashleigh's.

"On the count of three," Reena intoned, gripping the side of her backpack smashed beneath Vincent.

Nathan wanted to argue, but he didn't have a better plan. Getting into position, he carefully fed his hands between his niece's back and Vincent's front. The boy yowled and cringed, but he nodded for Reena to go.

"One. Two. Three."

Nathan lifted and everyone screamed, including him. Sweat poured from his hairline, mingling with the tears flowing freely. He had hurt his niece tremendously. It didn't matter he'd had to do it to save Vincent, he'd still caused her pain, and that wounded his soul.

Reena had managed to slide Vincent just far enough that Nathan could set Ashleigh back down in relatively the same place.

"I'm so sorry," he muttered over and over, kissing his niece's forehead.

Unzipping a side pocket on her backpack, Reena plucked out her cell phone. She held it up to the sun, then dropped her arm. "No signal."

He wanted to howl. "We need a medevac. *Now.*"

"I know." Her hand with the phone rested on her thigh

and she trembled all over. "I know." Wiping her sweaty forehead, she left a trail of blood behind.

His heart constricted. He had seen all the signs but only now did it hit him how much agony she must be in, too. "Reena."

"Stop. Don't say anything about my injuries." She snapped her gaze his way, her hazel eyes dull and glassy. "Ashleigh and Vincent are more important and in urgent condition."

Smoothing Ashleigh's forehead, Nathan scrabbled to figure out what to do.

"I'm going to head for the highway," Reena announced, pulling two socks out of the tight pocket on the side of her athletic shorts. She tucked the phone into the pocket and began working the white cotton over her hands. Blood immediately seeped into the fabric.

"You're in no condition for hiking," he argued, swallowing a lump in his throat from the fright and tears.

"It doesn't matter," she countered, wavering to her feet. "It's the only choice we have. We haven't seen anyone for days and I have no other way to signal for help."

"I—"

"We need help, not another argument," she snapped. "*You* have to stay here and protect the teens. Do what you can to keep them hydrated and whatever medical aid you can offer."

"Reena," he breathed. He didn't know what else to say. She was right, she had to go, but he *hated* it.

Studying him with an unreadable expression, she turned, and scrabbled off the boulder. Every thud, thump, yelp, and cry squeezed his heart until it barely beat.

Chapter Thirty-Three

Reena hugged the branch she'd found as a replacement walking stick and paused in the middle of the forest trail. Resting her forehead on the wood, she let go of the sob choking her breathing. She didn't have time to break down, but she needed to let the built-up pain go. She hurt to the point that she staggered instead of limped.

"God," she wheezed, "I need You to help me keep going. I can't make it without You. *Please*."

She had barely made it down the boulders, almost passing out twice, but she didn't stop. Limping as fast as she could for who knew how long had finally caught up to her.

"Please keep Nathan and the teens safe. They need You, too." Wiping the tears with her bloody socked hands, she forced one foot forward, then the other. Right boot and stick. Left boot. Repeat. If only she had gotten more sleep last night. She might have more energy now.

Fantasy. She would've used up that energy climbing the rocks—

Her knees slammed into the ground, then her palms. Hanging her head, she breathed hard. Drops of water plunked onto the path, her body wasting precious water on crying and sweat. She had fallen four times since she'd entered the woods and probably would buckle four more times before she reached help.

"Get up," she ordered her body. Her arm felt like a fifty-pound weight, but she managed to clamp on to her walking stick and drag it closer. Using the branch, it bowed to just shy of breaking, but it got her to her feet. Not bothering to wipe off the dirt and mud, she placed her right boot forward with the stick, then her left boot. Repeat.

The betrayal of Nathan, once again not trusting her, added to her agony. She knew how to navigate the forest, he didn't, yet he'd been about to say he would go. *Stop, Reena. Concentrate on the trail.*

Thick vegetation crowded closer and closer until the path disappeared. Using her stick, she pushed at branches and limbs, forcing them to part and, in some cases, untangle, so she could pass. Vines snagged her hair, tearing pieces out, and spiky twigs tore at her clothing. With blurry vision and hardly the ability to balance, she wove deeper into the mass. She lifted her stick, winding a throng of fragile branches around the end and stepped through—

"Ahh!" Her body thrust forward into air. Unable to stop herself, she tumbled downward. Sharp pokes and intense pain from wide-based hits assaulted her as she rolled end over end.

With one final turn, she landed in a river, her body half on a smooth rock, her upper half in the water.

The current pushed water over her head, holding it beneath the surface.

Roaring with fury and agony, she jammed her hands

on the rock and lifted. Pushing through the white foam, her cry suddenly blared off the surrounding trees. Thundering to her left had her blinking water from her eyelashes to focus on a…waterfall.

Whoa. A beautiful waterfall cascaded three stories over boulders to form watery steps. Amazing. With all the plants framing the falls, it looked like a magazine photo or nature advertisement.

"Ashleigh," she whispered, reminding herself why she had to push so hard. She couldn't linger or sightsee.

Without her stick, it took two tries to get to her feet. "Vincent."

Spying the break in the shrubs on the other side, she dunked her boots into the river. "Nathan."

They *needed* her to succeed. They *counted* on her not to fail.

The water rushed around her calves and tried to knock her down. The current ripped at her balance and she fought as hard as she could to keep going. Finally making it to the other side, she trudged up the slope to plunge back into the forest.

"Hurry." She tried to increase her pace.

Envisioning Ashleigh's broken leg, she coughed on barely catching her breath. Water mingled with the blood from new cuts and scratches as well as her existing ones.

"Move it."

Vincent's sallow skin as he'd struggled to put air in his lungs filled her mind. She couldn't stop, no matter how much she wanted to. *Needed* to.

Countless trees and shrubs passed. Clearings came and went. Deer, squirrels, rabbits, and raccoons bolted at her presence.

A huge black shadow loomed in front of her, startling

her. Veering left, she exhaled. She had almost run into an oak tree.

Focus, Reena.

Her eyes couldn't follow the command anymore. They remained blurry.

After an eternity, a brightness caught her attention and she lifted her gaze off the path. The tree line ended fifty feet ahead and she wanted to drop to her knees in relief. She'd made it. *Thank you, Lord.* She'd made it.

Pushing through the thick vegetation at the edge, she plopped onto the weedy grass beside a beautiful blacktop road. Listening hard, she didn't hear any cars, but her racing heart and rough breathing prevented her from hearing much. Her hand shook as she drew out her phone and she attempted to burst into fresh tears when she spied one bar in the signal indicator. Her dehydrated body couldn't provide the moisture.

Dialing 9-1-1, she put the phone on speaker. She didn't have the strength to hold it to her ear.

"Nine-one-one," a woman intoned. "What's your emergency?"

"Hello?" Reena cleared her throat, trying to force saliva into her mouth.

"Yes," the operator answered. "You've reached 9-1-1. What's your emergency?"

"My name is Reena Wells," she croaked as best she could. "We need your help."

Furious tapping on a keyboard ensued. "Did you say Reena Wells?"

"Yes." She couldn't hold herself upright anymore. Falling backward, she stared at the puffy clouds.

"You're the director of a teen youth group?" the operator asked.

Excitement pulsed in Reena's blood. "Yes."

The operator exhaled audibly. "Your church group reported you and three others missing yesterday afternoon."

A grin stole over Reena's face and she wheezed so hard she started hacking.

"I've pinged your location to the chief," the operator announced. "He's going to be so happy to hear you're safe—"

"Forget about me," Reena cut in. "We need a medevac ASAP."

"What happened?"

Reena described where Nathan, Ashleigh, and Vincent were and their conditions, ignoring the command for more details.

"Please," Reena pleaded. "Send the helicopter right away. I can tell you everything later. You have to get to them now."

Typing filled the background. "I know the boulder outcropping you're talking about." More typing. "The hospital has been alerted and they tell me a medevac is on its way."

"Thank you," she whispered.

"The chief is on his way to you…"

"I can't keep my eyes open anymore."

"Ma'am—"

That was the last thing Reena heard.

"Hey, there."

Reena snapped her gaze off the thin hospital sheet toward the male voice. "Vincent." She tried to smile but her face hurt. "You scared me to death. Again."

A pained grin grew as he shuffled from the doorway to her bedside.

Night had already fallen and she had been debating getting out of bed and searching for him and Ashleigh.

Reaching for his hand, she panted at the agony rushing through her body.

"Yeah." He obviously witnessed her working through the pain. "You won't be moving fast for a while."

"You're safe." Actual tears flowed down her cheeks and she swallowed around the lump in her throat. The hospital had been pumping her full of drugs and fluids for hours, restoring her hydration and fighting infection. "You're okay."

"Three fractured ribs and dehydration," he answered, clamping on to her arm near her elbow. "Warning. Mom's going to come by when she's finished talking to the doctor."

Reena's stomach clenched. "How mad is she?"

"At you?" He shifted, then flinched. "Not at all. In fact, she's so grateful you 'saved her son'—" he air quoted "—she's beside herself. But, me? She's beyond mad. Furious is more like it."

"You narc'ed on yourself?" Reena grinned, amazed at the teen's integrity.

"No way could I have her blame you when it was Ashleigh and I's fault we went swimming." He stretched his neck. "Anyway, has anybody told you anything about us?"

She carefully shook her head. "Privacy laws prevented the nurses from telling me if you guys even arrived at the hospital let alone how everyone was doing."

"We were picked up by a medevac," Vincent explained, "and rushed here. All three of us were placed on separate beds and whisked to different areas." He lowered into the ugly recliner beside the bed. "They've released me." He patted his chest gently. "The doctors taped me up and gave me pain pills."

"Ashleigh?" Reena wanted to ask about Nathan but couldn't bring herself to talk about him yet. She hadn't worked through everything that had happened between them.

"She'll be here for a while." He fingered the hem on a pair of scrubs the hospital must have supplied. "She just got out of surgery. It's bad." His body stiffened and he glared at the side of the bed. "Her right tibia is broken, she tore ligaments in her knee, and something to do with nerve damage." He adjusted his position. "Nathan's concussion has been diagnosed. He hasn't left Ashleigh for a single minute. From my understanding, he paced the waiting room like a caged tiger the entire time she was in surgery. I only saw him for a few minutes, but he looks like death warmed over."

"Thanks, Vincent." She rested one of her thickly bandaged palms on his hand. Both her hands were mummified, preventing her from doing much of anything.

"Hello." A perky nurse hustled into the room, pushing a small laptop cart in front of her. "Time to check your vitals." She began banging away on the poor keyboard. "Doctor's making his rounds now. If he likes what he sees, he'll release you in the morning."

Chapter Thirty-Four

"Vincent," Reena barked, sitting straighter on the tall stool. "Don't even *think* about lifting one of those."

The teen slowly took a step back from the first of a stack of folded easels resting against the back wall. "I want to help set up."

Saturday morning had come much quicker yet, in some ways, a lot slower than she'd expected. It had been a week since the worship-weekend-gone-wrong and she had been bumbling, relearning how to do the most basic things thanks to her overly bandaged hands. The large bruises decorating her skin had turned ugly colors and the cuts and scrapes were on the road to healing but still very much visible. Mother Nature had beaten her soundly.

She had stopped taking the pain pills the hospital provided within a day of arriving home. Now she wished she had popped one. She hadn't moved this much all week, but she wanted to be alert for the first day of class.

"Do I have to call your mother?" Reena asked, delivering the low blow to let Vincent know she meant business.

"That's just cruel." He pouted, his voice still laced

with a wheeze. He hadn't taken a full breath since last Sunday.

"But it got you to stop doing what you're not supposed to." Reena shifted to find a comfortable position for her still aching hips. In an hour, the first class in Intermediate Painting was set to begin at the community center. Students were supposed to have a basic understanding of painting but she wouldn't turn anyone away if they didn't. Normally, she'd be dashing around, setting up the stations, and arranging the necessary blank canvases, paint, and supplies. Unfortunately, she could only sit on her favorite stool in front of the room and hope the attendees didn't mind assembling their own stations once they arrived.

"I'm going to turn thirty before I'm out of the doghouse," Vincent grumped. He hid the tape wrapping his ribs underneath a paint-stained T-shirt hanging over basketball shorts. "Have you heard from—"

"Knock. Knock," a deep male tone stated from her right. She stiffened at the voice haunting her dreams, day and night.

Vincent's gaze shot to Reena. The man the teen had almost asked about stood in the doorway, but she didn't look that way. Not yet.

"Hi, Nathan," Vincent greeted. "Is it okay if I come over after my shift? It's my first day back to work, so my boss only scheduled me for two hours this afternoon."

Ashleigh had been released from the hospital two days ago. Vincent had told her how Nathan had rearranged the main floor of the house to accommodate her limitations and needs. Reena wanted to go see the teen in the worst way but hadn't been ready to talk to Nathan yet. Guess her time was up.

"Sure," Nathan agreed. "She's dying for company other than me. How are the ribs?"

"The same," Vincent replied, agitated. "They're taking *for-ever* to heal." Shuffling sounded. "Ashleigh owes me a rematch and I plan on winning this time."

A strained chuckle filled Reena's ears and she closed her eyes. To hear him again ignited so many emotions.

"Ashleigh takes the game of *Sorry!* seriously," Nathan warned. "She's whipped my butt too many times to count. I suggest finding something else to play."

"No way," Vincent retorted. "I'm going to beat her this time."

Rustling cloth and heavy boots drawing closer had Reena's eyelids snapping open. She stared at the easels so hard, she couldn't see them clearly anymore.

"Riiiight," Nathan drawled. "I wish you luck with that."

"Um." Vincent cleared his throat. "I'm going to, uh, see if anyone's arrived early." Another throat clear. "We'll stay in the lobby until, uh, you're ready, Reena."

She felt Vincent's absence immediately. Her stomach clenched and she bit her lip on a yelp when her hands tried to fist.

Nothing moved in the room for a tense fifteen seconds. Nathan finally broke the silence with a deep sigh. "You aren't even going to look at me?"

"I don't know," she answered honestly. She was afraid if she saw him, her heart would start making excuses, and she'd listen.

"Reena, I'm sorry."

The seriousness of his tone got her attention. "For what?" She wasn't going to assume anything. Wasn't that one of his complaints about her character?

Boot steps vibrated the floor and he blocked the stack

of easels. Nathan Porter did look like death warmed over, to use Vincent's description. His jeans hung low on his hips, held up by a sagging brown belt. A dark green polo with his company's logo was tucked in, but appeared loose on his normally muscular frame. He was still physically fit but somehow…diminished. Bruises covered large areas of his skin, and the bags under his eyes were tremendous. He had shaved off the scruff, and Reena blinked at the transformation. A strong jaw now showed clearly and a faint tan line appeared from where the hair had hidden his skin from the sun.

He needed a haircut. But bottom line? He looked beautiful and her soul still wanted to connect with him.

"I'm so sorry," he repeated hoarsely, his eyes roving her as much as hers did to him. "Are you okay—"

"Why are you here, Nathan?" She cut him off. She hadn't seen him since she'd left him on the boulder. Not once had he visited or contacted her.

He winced. "I deserve that." Bruised knuckles flashed as he swiped through his hair, then he pierced her with dark brown eyes filled with sorrow and…anxiety? "I didn't come to see you before because I needed time to process everything that happened last weekend."

Sock to the gut. What did he mean by that?

His pupils widened and he pulled on his hair. "That didn't come out right." He paced to the side windows and back. "I knew I'd screw this up," he muttered.

"Just tell me why you're here," Reena repeated, hardening her heart wanting to reach for him. It hurt so much to see him, hear him.

"To apologize." He stopped in front of her stool. The amazing scent of his musk assaulted her senses and she inhaled like a lovesick fool.

"You said that." Reena tried to take shallow breaths to keep her mind clear. "For what are you apologizing?"

"So much," he rasped on an exhale, inching closer. "I *wanted* to see you. I got in my truck dozens of times and had my finger poised over your name in my phone contacts."

"But…"

"I didn't know what to say." Another inch closer. "So much happened in such a short period of time." He blew out a breath. "When Ashleigh fell, I made promises to God, who I've been so angry with. Promises I meant at the time but, after the fact, wasn't sure I could keep." He turned to look out the side windows. "Since the day Scott died, I've been furious. That he'd take Ashleigh's father from her after already claiming her mother. That He'd force me to move my life to Bell Edge and care for a teenager when I had no clue what to do."

His fingers resting against his hips whitened.

Reena kept silent.

He sighed so hard, his chest deflated. "But I started to see things different." He flicked his gaze her way. "You had a lot to do with that. Our conversation on the trail made me see that I had to be doing something right. Ashleigh's healthy and living life. It was *me* who hadn't been dealing with Scott's death." His boot shuffled on the tile. "It took Ashleigh's accident for me to wake up and see all that God has given me and all the ways He's helped me. And it's hard, but I'm committed to keeping my promises to God."

"I'm so glad to hear this, Nathan." Reena's heart pounded but she quickly regained control. "I truly am, but you could have told me at church tomorrow."

He nodded, then turned to face her. "I also had to

make sure what I felt for you was real and not in the moment."

Reena's lungs froze.

He closed the distance and hovered his palms above her bandaged hands resting on her thighs. "You're beautiful. Inside and out."

She couldn't move, his words and gaze held her captive.

"I noticed you the second I walked into church six months ago," he continued softly, his hands still above hers. "But I started falling for you when you strapped on your backpack and didn't hesitate to look for the teens in the middle of an epic thunderstorm. Dragging my contrary butt along with you on top of that."

Black spots edged her vision and she forced herself to inhale.

He peered at her bandages, then roved his gaze over her once more. "You amaze me." A light brush on her forearm startled her. "Despite all your injuries, you kept charging forward, determined to find a way off the mountain." His eyes lowered and remained on her stiff hands. "And I didn't have the intelligence to trust you."

Tears formed at the corners of her eyes. He understood the core of the pain he'd caused.

Lifting his gaze, he met hers. "I should have trusted you, Reena." The pad of his forefinger wiped a tear off her cheek. "Last weekend and this week has opened my eyes *a lot*." He curled his hand into a fist. "I've missed you so much, it's scary."

She'd missed him, too. So, so much, at times she couldn't breathe.

"I should've also trusted Ashleigh once we found her and Vincent," he confessed softly. "It pains my ego to say this, but I can't control everything." He smirked. "I can't secure my niece in bubble wrap to stop every bad thing from happening to her. It's not healthy for either of us, and I have to stop thinking like that. You were right. I'll lose her if I don't loosen my grip and let her make and learn from her own mistakes."

Reena want to *whoop!* but her voice stayed locked in her throat.

"But I'll need help with that," he continued. "*Tons* of help."

Was he…asking her to help him?

"Reena." He captured another tear. "It's not right that I blamed you for everything that went wrong. I'm sorry. I'm sorrier than you'll ever know. I should have trusted your recommendation when we got to the crossroads." Anguish rounded his shoulders. "It's all my fault. It could take Ashleigh a year or more to walk normally again. *My* decision did that to her." Tears filled his eyes. "And Vincent's sporting fractured ribs because of me." He shuddered. "It's my fault your palms are so injured you have to wear these bandages, and those bruises covering your body—"

"Stop," she ordered, her voice croaking. "There's no way to know if the path I chose would have turned out any different. Mine had a wall that could have just as easily caused the same thing to happen."

"Don't make excuses for me." He stepped back, blinking hard. Not a tear fell.

"I'm not." Reena slid off the tall stool. Flinching at her hips and muscles jarring with the motion. "Can I ask a question?"

"Anything."

She searched his face, spying the wariness and hope warring. "You admit to falling for me." Repeating those words out loud hit her hard. "But, do you honestly believe you can trust me to help you with Ashleigh, knowing I'm probably going to push for something that goes against your instincts? Do you honestly believe you can trust me to make hard decisions going forward?"

"Yes," he whispered without hesitation. "I have so many examples bursting on the tip of my tongue. You've already proven you're trustworthy, and I'm an exceedingly stupid man for not seeing them until after I hurt you."

She blinked at the renewed tears filling her vision. "What about my sunny outlook on life? My 'happy, happy, joy, joy,' you called it. That's not going to change."

"And I'm surprisingly glad of that." A small smile twitched the left side of his mouth and his dark brown eyes lightened. "In an irony I now find funny." He gently lifted her left hand and held it in his palm. "I once described Ashleigh's and Vincent's different personalities as complementing each other, making them perfect together."

Light filled her heavy soul, chasing out the dark sorrow confining it for days. "Opposite qualities can mix together harmoniously like the colors red and blue making purple."

"Exactly." He cupped her cheek with his free hand. "We make purple."

If her grin beaming at him was as goofy as the one on his face, Reena couldn't help it. "I have a confession to make."

His fingers stiffened. "You do?" he whispered.

"I started falling for you, too," Reena blurted.

"Hallelujah!" he crowed, his sudden radiance blinding her.

"Do you have any interest in a relationship that could lead to a lifelong partnership?" Reena took the plunge. "We can work on important stuff such as *making,* not avoiding, conversation at church, and understanding that cupcakes are the best junk food—"

"Yes!" Nathan shouted, laughing at the same time. "You, Ms. Sunshine, have me inexplicably believing that sometimes the unexpected twists in life are better than anything I can plan for."

* * * * *

"He's brazen. He parked right behind Izzy's old van knowing there was a possibility of someone—maybe even me—seeing it." Which she had. She could kick herself for not getting the tag number.

"Are you saying I'm looking for an arrogant killer who loves the thrill of almost getting caught but believes he won't because he's uncatchable?"

Her past mistakes told her not to make a solid conclusion so soon, but this guy had proven more than once what kind of man he was, what kind of killer. Still, she hesitated to give Tack a profile that would aid in his search. "Perhaps," she said as a knot pinched in her gut.

"Perhaps? Chelsey, give me something I can work with."

Chelsey drank the ice water, letting it cool her burning throat. What if she was wrong? "I'm not ready to spin what little thread we have into a tapestry yet." She could not have another profile backfiring. Another stain on her previously impeccable record. Lives depended on it. Tack's career depended on it. The last thing Chelsey wanted was Tack's name being smeared because of his connection with Chelsey and her profession.

Or her personal stains that could smear him.

"Agents—" a hospital security officer stepped inside "—we have a media frenzy outside. They want more information on this Outlaw. They know a woman died at his hands. In our care."

The Outlaw. Chelsey's name for him.

The only other person besides Tack who knew she'd called him that was Juan. He must have talked to the press after he left the hospital. So much for not letting their personal nickname for him get out. Now they were here wanting answers. She didn't have a single one.

"We're going to have to go out there, Chels," Tack said. "Me and you. Working a case together. Who would have thought?"

And now if anything at all were amiss, Tack would go down with an already sinking ship, in the form of his oldest and dearest friend.

What had she gotten him into? And could she get him out?

Don't miss
Texas Cold Case Threat *by Jessica R. Patch,*
available March 2022 wherever
Love Inspired Suspense books and ebooks are sold.

And look for a new extended-length novel from
Jessica R. Patch, Her Darkest Secret,
coming soon from Love Inspired!

LoveInspired.com

Get 4 FREE REWARDS!

We'll send you 2 FREE Books plus 2 FREE Mystery Gifts.

Love Inspired Suspense books showcase how courage and optimism unite in stories of faith and love in the face of danger.

FREE Value Over **$20**
